From the BookFest 2026 3rd Place–Winning Romance Series

She Came at the Glass Heel
Book 1

First Step

Tatiana Vixen Reyes

First Step
Copyright © 2025 Tatiana Vixen Reyes
Published by Velvet Orchid Press

ISBN (ebook): 979-8-9997682-0-9
ISBN (paperback): 979-8-9997682-4-7

Cover design by Aleksandar (@blokowsky on Fiverr)

This series was awarded 3rd Place in the
Romance – Series category at The Book Fest (2026).

www.velvetorchidpress.com
www.tatianavixenreyes.com

For all transgender people taking
that first step into the world as
who they truly are.

Chapter 1

The Threshold

The night swallowed her footsteps, each one a hesitation as the snow dusted her shoulders like a cold benediction.

Claire counted the steps between streetlamps, her berry-stained lips mouthing the numbers as if they might form a convincing argument against continuing. Twelve steps, thirteen, fourteen—each one carrying her closer to The Glass Heel, each one a decision she could still unmake. The invitation card burned in her coat pocket, its embossed lettering catching against her fingertips whenever she reached for it to confirm, yet again, the address.

I could just go home.

The thought arrived like a friend offering a warm blanket. Her apartment was only fifteen minutes back— fifteen minutes to safety, to invisibility, to the familiar ache of almost. Snowflakes caught in her eyelashes, blurring the world into soft, forgiving edges.

"My feet hurt," she whispered to no one, testing the excuse aloud. The kitten heels she'd chosen pinched at the toes, still new enough to bite. "I could call it practice. Just getting outside was the victory."

A couple passed, huddled together against the cold, the woman's laughter rising like steam. Claire tucked her chin deeper into her scarf, angling her face away. Did they notice? Did they see? Her pulse quickened beneath the wool.

Another block passed beneath her uncertain steps. The snow was falling faster now, gathering at the hems of her coat. She glanced down at her stockings, already dampening from the flurries.

"I should have checked the weather," Claire murmured, imagining her makeup beginning to run. Two hours of painstaking work—the foundation, the contouring, the subtle shadow that made her eyes look wider, more feminine—all of it dissolving in the winter moisture. Her reflection in a darkened storefront window confirmed her fears: a smudge beneath her right eye, mascara threatening to streak.

"This is a sign," she told herself, relief and disappointment warring in her chest. "I'm not ready. Not tonight."

The Glass Heel was just ahead now, its black awning and subtle gold insignia barely visible through the thickening snow. A small line had formed outside, women in glittering dresses huddled together beneath umbrellas, laughing despite the cold. Beautiful women. Real women.

Claire's throat tightened. Her hand drifted to her neck, fingers pressing against the smooth skin where her Adam's apple had been reduced but not erased. Would they see it immediately? Would the bouncer know?

"I forgot my ID," she whispered, patting her clutch as if to confirm the lie. But no—her fingers found the hard edge of her driver's license, the one with her new name, the photo she'd agonized over for weeks.

A taxi pulled up to the curb, its yellow brightness spilling across the snow. Claire stepped back into the shadows and was suddenly back in her apartment three hours earlier, standing before the open closet doors.

"What was I thinking?" Claire whispered, letting her fingertips wander over the hanging fabrics. The black dress she'd ordered online hung untouched, tags still in place—a simple sheath with three-quarter sleeves and a modest neckline. Safe. Unremarkable. Next to it, the emerald silk caught the lamp's glow, rippling like liquid jade, its drape more sensuous, more daring.

Her pulse fluttered as she lifted the emerald gown from its hanger. Bought on a moment of reckless hope six months ago, it had never left her closet. Now she pressed the cool silk to her skin and studied her reflection in the full-length mirror, watching the gown hug curves she barely recognized.

"Too much," she murmured, yet she couldn't bear to return it.

In the bathroom the overhead bulb cast harsh shadows across her cheeks and deepened the hollow beneath her eyes. She squeezed her foundation sponge with trembling fingers. She'd memorized dozens of tutorials, phone perched on the sink, but every movement felt clumsy. The first layer spread unevenly, accentuating the faint shadow of stubble instead of covering it. With a ragged breath, she blotted it away and began again.

"Blend outward," she coached herself, mimicking the YouTuber's calming tone. "Small circles. Build slowly."

Her lids stung as she drew a trembling line of eyeliner; it smeared before she could finish. Mascara clumped her lashes into sticky tufts. Lipstick bled beyond her lip line in a messy halo. Claire exhaled, pressing her palms into the cold sink to steady herself.

"I can't do this," she whispered. The face staring back was a stranger's—half-formed, caught between two worlds. She dragged a tissue across her mouth; the berry stain blurred into an ugly smear.

After nearly an hour, the counter was a battlefield: cotton rounds soaked in makeup remover, crumpled tissues, brushes splayed like abandoned weapons. The YouTube tutorial continued in the background: "For a more dramatic evening look, intensify the crease color and blend upward…"

Trembling, Claire swirled an eyeshadow brush in glittering powder. A burst of color scattered across her cheekbone like shattered stardust. Tears welled as she met her own gaze.

"Who are you trying to fool?" she demanded. The mirror offered no mercy—only the truth of her square jaw, broad shoulders, and long fingers clutching the brush as if it might break.

She'd restarted her routine three times. Her phone read 8:45 PM. Doors opened at The Glass Heel at 9:00. A forty-five-minute ride on the L and a fifteen-minute walk lay between her and the night she'd dreamed of. Time and courage slipped through her trembling hands.

The taxi door slammed, bringing Claire sharply back to the present. She pressed herself deeper into the shadow of the awning, watching as three women emerged from the cab. They were laughing, touching each other's arms, fixing each other's collars—so comfortable in their bodies, in their belonging.

Claire's stomach clenched. The emerald dress beneath her coat suddenly felt like a costume, something she'd stolen rather than earned. She tugged at the hem through her coat pocket, feeling the delicate silk bunch between her fingers.

They'll know. The second I walk in, they'll see through me.

Her reflection in the dark window beside her was a ghost—a smudge of a person half-formed, half-present. How many years had she spent like this? Hovering at thresholds, watching others move through the world with such easy grace while she remained trapped in the liminal spaces, neither here nor there.

The hormones had softened her face, redistributed the weight on her hips, but they couldn't erase the map of her origins. Her hands—those betraying hands—were still too large, the knuckles too pronounced. She shoved them deep into her pockets.

I don't fit in here, she mused, observing a man and a woman as they joined the queue. I'm just a shadow trying to pass as a human.

The bouncer was checking IDs now, his broad shoulders blocking the doorway as he studied each card. Claire imagined him looking at hers, at the photograph taken six months ago, the "F" newly printed beside "Sex." Would he notice the subtle mismatch between the picture and her face tonight? Would his eyes narrow in that familiar way?

"Last chance," she whispered to herself, already turning to leave.

But her gaze caught on the couple ahead—the woman leaned into her partner, whispering something that made him laugh. The sound was warm, genuine. Something about their ease tugged at Claire, an ache of longing so fierce it momentarily overshadowed her fear.

Before she could reconsider, Claire stepped forward. One step, then another, her kitten heels clicking against the wet pavement. She positioned herself behind the couple, close enough to catch the woman's perfume— something with vanilla and amber. Her heart thundered so loudly she was certain they could hear it.

The line moved forward. Claire's fingers found the invitation in her pocket again, tracing its embossed edges. The couple ahead murmured to each other, oblivious to her internal chaos. Three more people ahead now. Two. One.

Then it was her turn.

The bouncer's face was impassive, framed by a neat beard. His eyes—dark, evaluating—met hers. Claire's throat tightened as she withdrew her ID with trembling fingers, passing it over. The plastic felt slick in her sweaty palm.

He studied it longer than he had the others. Or was that her imagination? The seconds stretched, elastic with terror. Claire felt a trickle of sweat slide down her back despite the frigid air.

"Glass Heel, huh?" the bouncer said, passing the ID back to her. His voice was neutral, impossible to read. "You been here before?"

"No," Claire said, the word barely a whisper. She cleared her throat and tried again. "No, first time."

Something in his expression softened, almost imperceptibly. "Welcome, then." He stepped aside, pulling open the heavy door. "Mind the step."

Claire blinked, frozen in momentary disbelief. That was it? No questions, no suspicious glances, no—

"Miss?" The bouncer raised an eyebrow. "You heading in?"

"Yes. Sorry." She tucked her ID away and moved forward, heart hammering against her ribs as she crossed the threshold.

The door closed behind her with a soft thud, sealing away the winter night. Claire stood motionless in the entryway, her senses overwhelmed by the sudden transformation of her world. The club unfurled before her like a velvet dream. Crimson candles flickered in crystal holders along the bar, their flames dancing in tempo with the low, pulsing beat that seemed to emanate from the walls themselves. Claire's eyes struggled to adjust to the amber glow that bathed everything in honeyed warmth, transforming ordinary features into something otherworldly. The music wasn't loud—not the deafening thump she'd feared—but rather a rhythmic heartbeat that vibrated through the soles of her shoes, inviting rather than demanding.

To her right, curved booths of deep sapphire velvet lined the wall, each one a private universe unto itself. Women lounged against the plush backs, their bodies arranged like Renaissance paintings—all curves and shadows, light catching on exposed shoulders and the rims of cocktail glasses. A woman with cropped silver hair threw her head back in laughter, her throat a perfect column in the candlelight.

Claire pressed herself against the wall, suddenly aware of her coat, still buttoned to her chin. Everyone else had shed their outer layers, revealing dresses that clung and flowed, suits tailored to feminine curves, bodies unashamed of the space they occupied.

"Can I take your coat?"

Claire startled at the voice beside her. A young person with a cloud of dark curls and wine-colored lipstick held out their hand, smiling.

"Here, let me help you." The coat check attendant stepped closer, gently assisting with the last stubborn button that Claire's trembling fingers couldn't manage.

"Thank you," Claire whispered, slipping the heavy wool from her shoulders. The emerald silk of her dress caught the light as she surrendered her coat, exposing her bare arms to the warm air of the club. Her skin prickled with vulnerability.

"Beautiful dress," the attendant said, their eyes appreciative rather than evaluating. They handed Claire a small brass token. "Keep this safe."

Claire nodded, sliding the ticket into her clutch. The absence of her coat left her feeling exposed, as if she'd shed armor before battle. She drew a deep breath, inhaling the mingled scents of perfume, candle wax, and something deeper—desire, perhaps, or freedom.

The bar beckoned like a sanctuary, its polished surface gleaming under strategically placed lights. Claire made her way toward it, each step measured, careful. She counted them silently—one, two, three—focusing on the rhythm to quiet the thunder of her pulse.

Behind the bar, a man with dark curls pulled back into a short ponytail poured amber liquid into a tumbler. His movements were fluid, precise, like a dancer who knew every step by muscle memory. As Claire approached, he looked up, his deep-set eyes meeting hers with quiet attention.

"What can I get you?" His voice was low, resonant, without the judgment Claire had braced herself to hear.

"Um..." She scanned the bottles behind him, her mind suddenly blank. "Something... sweet? But not too sweet."

He nodded, studying her face with a gentleness that made her want to look away. "First time here?"

"Is it that obvious?" The words escaped before she could trap them.

His lips curved into a small smile. "Only because I know all the regulars." He reached for a bottle with an amber liquid. "I'm Julian. Let me make you something that'll help with those nerves."

Claire watched his hands as he worked—confident, steady hands with a small tattoo on the inside of his wrist. Something in his calm presence made her shoulders lower slightly from where they'd been hovering near her ears.

"Thank you," she murmured as he slid a glass toward her. The liquid inside was the color of honey, garnished with a twist of orange peel.

"On the house," Julian said, his eyes kind. "Welcome to The Glass Heel."

Claire fumbled in her clutch. "No, please, I can—"

"First drink's always on the house for newcomers. House rules." He nodded toward her glass. "It's a whiskey sour with a twist—sweet but not cloying."

Claire lifted the glass, taking a tentative sip. The flavor bloomed across her tongue—bright citrus and warmth, with just enough bite to be interesting.

"It's perfect. Thank you." She took another sip, longer this time, letting the alcohol's warmth spread through her chest.

Julian nodded and moved down the bar to attend to another patron, leaving Claire to survey the room. The Glass Heel hummed with energy—beautiful bodies in motion, conversations flowing like water. Everyone seemed to belong, to know exactly who they were and why they were here.

Claire clutched her glass and moved toward an empty corner at the far end of the bar. The shadows there were deeper, offering a pocket of relative privacy from which to observe. She slid onto a high stool, arranging her dress carefully beneath her, conscious of how the silk caught the light.

From her shadowed corner, Claire caught a glimpse of movement in the mirror behind the bar—a flash of crimson that drew her eye like a flame. She froze, glass halfway to her lips, as the reflection materialized into a woman. Not just any woman—a vision in red that seemed to part the crowd without touching it.

The woman wore a floor-length gown the color of spilled wine, the fabric clinging to curves that seemed sculpted rather than born. Her dark hair was swept up in an elegant chignon that exposed the long column of her neck, adorned with a single gold pendant that caught the light with each breath she took. The gown's neckline plunged daringly low, revealing olive skin that glowed in the amber light.

Claire couldn't look away. Through the safety of the mirror, she watched as the woman in crimson moved through the club with predatory grace, her gaze sweeping the room as if searching for something—or someone. There was purpose in her movements, a focused intensity that made Claire's breath catch.

The whiskey sour turned bitter on Claire's tongue. This woman was everything she wasn't—confident, striking, unquestionably feminine. She possessed the kind of beauty that didn't need to announce itself; it simply commanded attention.

"Breathe," Claire whispered to herself, setting down her glass with trembling fingers. She smoothed her emerald dress, suddenly aware of its modest cut, the way it hung slightly wrong across her shoulders.

"I see you've found my favorite spot for watching."

A voice, warm as spiced honey, startled Claire from her fixation. She turned to find a woman standing beside her—not the crimson-clad vision from the mirror, but someone equally magnetic in a completely different way.

The woman was tall, regal in her bearing, with raven-black hair arranged in vintage rolls that framed a face both striking and serene. Her custom-tailored dress flowed around her like liquid shadow, and around her neck hung a single glass heel pendant that caught the light with each breath. Her smile held secrets, promises, and something that felt startlingly like recognition.

"I—I'm sorry," Claire stammered, her fingers tightening around her glass. "I didn't mean to take someone's spot."

"No apologies needed in my house," the woman said, sliding onto the stool beside Claire with effortless grace. "I'm Echo Dela Cruz. This is my establishment."

Claire felt heat rise to her cheeks. The owner. Of course. She'd stumbled into the owner's private corner like a lost child.

"I can move," she offered, already gathering her clutch.

Echo's hand, warm and steady, settled briefly on Claire's wrist. "Stay. Please." The touch was light as a butterfly, there and gone in an instant, but it anchored Claire to the spot. "First time at The Glass Heel?"

Echo's gaze swept over Claire with a gentle intensity that somehow felt like being wrapped in velvet.

"Your first visit," she said, not a question but a quiet affirmation. "I make it my business to know every face that walks through these doors."

Claire swallowed hard, acutely aware of the woman's presence beside her—the subtle perfume of sandalwood and something darker, the way the shadows seemed to bend toward her rather than away.

"Yes," Claire managed. "My first time."

Echo's lips curved into a smile that held warmth without pity. "And you chose to observe before participating. Wise." She signaled to Julian without looking away from Claire. "Another for our new friend, please. Something with a bit more courage in it."

"I still have this one," Claire protested weakly, lifting her half-empty glass.

"But you need something different now." Echo's voice was soft but left no room for argument. "The first drink at The Glass Heel is for arrival. The second is for becoming."

Julian appeared with two glasses of amber liquid, neat, with a twist of lemon peel. He set them down without comment and disappeared again, efficient as a shadow.

"Thank you," Claire murmured, uncertain if she was thanking Echo or Julian or both.

Echo lifted her glass in a small toast. "To thresholds crossed."

Claire mirrored the gesture, her hand steadier than she expected. The whiskey burned pleasantly as it went down, warming Claire from the inside. She glanced at Echo, who was studying her with those penetrating brown eyes.

"Let me guess," Echo said, resting one elegant finger against her glass. "You spent at least an hour debating whether to come tonight. Probably walked past the door once or twice before finally deciding to enter."

Claire nearly choked on her drink. "How did you—"

"The Glass Heel tends to attract seekers," Echo said, her voice a melodic hum against the club's ambient music. "Those standing at a crossroads. I've welcomed thousands through that door, and I recognize the look of someone who's just taken a leap of faith." She tilted her head, the glass heel pendant catching the light. "What's your name?"

"Claire," she answered, her own name feeling new on her tongue in this space.

"Claire," Echo repeated, as if tasting the syllables. "It

suits you. Open and clear, but with hidden depths."

The compliment settled over Claire like a warm shawl. She took another sip of whiskey, finding her voice. "Have you owned this place long?"

Echo's laugh was soft smoke. "Long enough to watch women walk in as strangers to themselves and leave as something more." She shifted on her stool, angling her body toward Claire with undivided attention. "Tell me, what brought you to my door tonight?"

The question hung between them, deceptively simple. Claire stared into her glass, watching the light refract through the amber liquid. What had brought her here? The invitation card with its embossed lettering? The desperate need to be somewhere—anywhere—where she might not feel like an impostor in her own skin?

"I'm not sure I know," Claire admitted, surprising herself with her honesty.

Echo nodded as if this were the most reasonable answer in the world. "The best journeys often begin that way." She leaned closer, her voice dropping to a confidential murmur. "Would you like to know a secret, Claire?"

The way Echo said her name—with such easy familiarity—made something loosen in Claire's chest. She nodded.

"Everyone you see here tonight arrived exactly as you did: hearts racing, palms sweating, wondering if they'd made a terrible mistake." Echo's gaze swept across the room, affection warming her features. "Even that woman in the red dress you were watching so intently."

Claire's cheeks burned. "I wasn't—"

Echo's laugh was warm velvet. "The mirrors in this place reveal more than reflections, dear one. Elena was once where you are now. First night, corner seat, watching everyone else belong."

"Elena," Claire repeated softly, the name a revelation. Not just a vision in crimson, but a person with a name.

"What do you do, Claire, when you're not gathering courage in bars?" Echo asked, seamlessly shifting the conversation.

The question caught Claire off guard with its normalcy. It was the kind of question strangers asked at dinner parties, not in velvet-draped nightclubs while sipping whiskey.

"I'm a graphic designer," she said, surprised by the steadiness in her voice. "Mostly freelance work for small businesses. Logos, websites, that sort of thing."

Echo nodded appreciatively. "A creator of identities. How fitting." She gestured toward Claire's emerald dress. "You have an eye for color. That shade is remarkable against your skin."

The compliment bloomed warm in Claire's chest. She ran her fingers along the silk, allowing herself to feel its luxury. "Thank you. I've had it for months but never worn it until tonight."

"And why tonight?" Echo's question was gentle but direct, her eyes never leaving Claire's face.

Claire took another sip of whiskey, letting the burn fortify her. "Because keeping it in my closet felt like... like admitting defeat." The words came unbidden, surprising her with their honesty.

Echo's smile deepened, crinkling the corners of her eyes. "Ah, so you're a fighter."

"I don't feel like one most days."

"The bravest warriors rarely do." Echo shifted, angling her body to create a pocket of privacy in the bustling club. "Tell me about your art. What draws you to design?"

Claire hesitated, warmth creeping up her neck. No one had asked about her work with such genuine interest in months. "I love how design can communicate without words. The right curves, the perfect color—they speak directly to something inside us."

Echo leaned forward, as if Claire's words were precious gems she didn't want to miss. "That's exactly what I aimed for with The Glass Heel. A visual language that speaks to the soul before the mind catches up." She gestured around them with a fluid movement of her wrist. "The lighting, the textures—they tell you you're safe before anyone says a word."

"You succeeded," Claire admitted, surprising herself with her candor. "When I walked in, before the panic hit, there was this moment of... exhaling."

"That exhale is everything," Echo said, her voice dropping to a confidential murmur. "It's the sound of armor falling away." She studied Claire's face, not with judgment but with a kind of tender curiosity. "You've been wearing yours for quite some time, haven't you?"

The question should have felt invasive, but something about Echo's presence made it feel like care. Claire took another sip of whiskey, letting the warmth spread through her chest.

"Most of my life," she answered softly.

Echo nodded as if Claire had confirmed something she already knew. "The heaviest burdens are the ones we've carried so long we forget they're not part of us." She touched her glass heel pendant, the light playing across its crystalline edges. "Perhaps tonight is about setting down what no longer serves you."

Echo's words settled into Claire like a truth she'd always known but never named. The whiskey had loosened something in her chest, making it easier to breathe in this velvet-dark space where everyone seemed to be exactly who they were meant to be.

"What if I don't know who I am without it?" Claire asked, the question barely audible above the music.

Echo's smile deepened, her eyes reflecting the candlelight. "That's the beauty of The Glass Heel, Claire. It's a place between worlds—where you can try on different versions of yourself and see which ones fit." She leaned closer, her voice dropping to a conspiratorial whisper. "The night has a way of answering questions you haven't even thought to ask yet."

Claire felt a shiver run down her spine, not of fear but anticipation.

"When you look in the mirror tonight," Echo continued, her fingers brushing Claire's wrist with butterfly lightness, "try to see what others see when they look at you, not what your fears tell you they see." She rose from her stool with fluid grace, the movement drawing eyes from across the bar. "Open yourself to possibility, Claire. The most beautiful transformations happen when we stop fighting what we might become."

Echo turned to leave, but paused and looked back with a slight smile. "Just one more thing, Claire." She moved closer, her breath softly brushing Claire's ear. "The women who end up here are searching for something they can't quite define. But the night has a knack for uncovering exactly what we need, even if we're hesitant to express it." She gave Claire's hand a gentle squeeze. "Trust that feeling when it comes. That magnetic draw toward someone else? It's the universe working for your benefit."

With that, Echo slipped away into the crowd, her silhouette dissolving among the dancers like smoke. Claire watched her go, Echo's words settling into her bones like a promise—or perhaps a warning.

Claire turned back to her drink, fingers tracing the cool rim of the glass. Trust the pull. She took a slow sip, the whiskey no longer burning but warming her from within. The amber light of the bar caught in the crystal tumbler, fracturing into tiny stars against the polished wood.

Claire turns to look at the mirror behind the bar, searching for Elena. She doesn't spot her at first, but she suddenly realizes that she is standing right behind her.

Chapter 2

A Stranger Who Sees Her

"I've been watching you for twenty minutes, wondering what kind of courage it takes to sit alone at the edge of a room full of strangers."

Claire's hand froze around her glass, the whiskey suddenly heavy as lead in her stomach. The voice behind her was warm honey poured over gravel—rich and textured with just enough roughness to catch the ear. She turned slowly, her heart hammering against her ribs like a trapped bird.

Elena stood there, crimson silk cascading around her body as if painted by an artist's careful hand. Up close, she was even more striking—warm bronze skin that seemed to glow from within, deep brown eyes framed by lashes that curled naturally without mascara's assistance, and full lips curved into a smile that held no judgment, only curiosity.

"I'm Elena," she said, extending a hand adorned with

a single gold ring. No excessive jewelry, no desperate grab for attention—just the quiet confidence of someone who had nothing to prove. "May I join you?"

Claire nodded, not trusting her voice. Her fingers trembled slightly as they met Elena's, the touch sending an electric current up her arm. Elena's hand was warm and dry, her grip firm but gentle.

"Thank you," Elena said, sliding onto the stool Echo had vacated minutes earlier. She moved with an unhurried grace, as if time itself bent to accommodate her rhythm. "And you are?"

"Claire," she managed, the word coming out softer than intended.

"Claire," she repeated, her voice like crushed velvet. "A beautiful name."

Elena settled beside her with the ease of someone who belonged everywhere and nowhere at once. She didn't fidget or adjust her dress, just folded her hands in her lap and turned toward Claire with unhurried attention. The crimson silk of her dress caught the light when she moved, creating shadows that danced across her collarbone.

"I hope I'm not intruding," Elena said. Her accent was barely perceptible—something Mediterranean perhaps, softening her consonants. "But in a place like this, solitude is usually either a shield or an invitation."

Claire's throat tightened. Which was she? She hadn't thought of her corner seat as either protection or welcome, but suddenly both possibilities seemed equally true.

"I'm not sure which one I am," she admitted, surprising herself with her honesty.

Elena's laugh was low and warm, like a hand pressed against the small of Claire's back. "The fact that you're still here talking to me suggests you might be a little of both." She gestured to Julian without looking away from Claire's face. "Would you allow me to buy you another?"

Claire glanced at her nearly empty glass, not remembering when she'd finished it. "I should probably slow down."

"Then perhaps some water?" Elena suggested, her concern so natural it didn't feel like judgment. "The night is young, and The Glass Heel has many secrets worth staying clear-headed for."

Julian appeared with a glass of water, setting it down with a nod before disappearing again. Claire reached for it gratefully, using the moment to gather her thoughts.

"So," she began, wincing inwardly at how flat the word sounded. "Do you come here often?" The moment the cliché left her lips, Claire wanted to sink into the floor. Her cheeks burned. "I mean—that wasn't—I don't usually—"

"Yes," Elena answered simply, rescuing her from the stumbling explanation. "The Glass Heel feels like home to me now. But there was a time when I stood outside for nearly an hour before finding the courage to enter." Her smile held no mockery, only understanding.

Claire took another sip of water, desperately searching for something intelligent to say. "The... the music is nice." She gestured vaguely toward the dance floor, where bodies moved in sensual rhythm.

"It is," Elena agreed, her gaze steady, still fixed on Claire. "Heather's our regular DJ—she reads the room like a lover. Her playlists shift every hour, just enough to keep you breathing in time with the beat."

Silence stretched between them. Claire fidgeted with her glass, tracing the condensation with her fingertip. "I'm terrible at this," she confessed, the words tumbling out before she could stop them.

"At what?" Elena asked, her head tilting slightly.

"Talking. To people. To women." Claire's voice dropped to a whisper on the last word. "Especially beautiful women."

Elena's expression remained warm, her eyes never leaving Claire's face. "I think you're doing just fine."

"That's kind of you to say, but..." Claire swallowed, her fingers still tracing circles on the condensation of her water glass. "I feel like I'm floundering."

"May I tell you a secret?" Elena leaned forward slightly, her voice dropping to a conspiratorial murmur. "Most conversation is just that—floundering elegantly until we find common ground."

Claire's laugh escaped before she could trap it, a small surprised sound that seemed to please Elena, whose smile deepened at the corners.

"So," Elena continued, "tell me something about yourself that has nothing to do with why you're here tonight."

Claire blinked, caught off-guard by the simplicity of the request. "I... I have a cat named Pixel. She's completely black except for one white paw that looks like she stepped in paint."

"A perfect name for her, then. Are you a photographer?"

"Graphic designer," Claire corrected, feeling the familiar ground of her profession steady her slightly. "Freelance mostly. I work from home, which Pixel appreciates because it means constant lap access."

Elena nodded, her attention so focused that Claire almost forgot they were in a crowded club. "Working from home can be both liberating and isolating. Do you enjoy it?"

"Most days," Claire said, warming to the subject. "I

like being able to work in my own space. Create my own schedule." Claire's fingers relaxed around her glass, the rhythm of conversation becoming easier. "Though sometimes I miss having coworkers to bounce ideas off of."

"I understand completely," Elena said, her gaze momentarily drifting to the dance floor where bodies moved in fluid synchronicity. "Would you like to sit somewhere more comfortable? Those booths look inviting."

Claire followed Elena's gaze to the sapphire velvet booths lining the far wall. The intimate seating suddenly seemed both terrifying and irresistible.

"Yes," she heard herself say. "That would be nice."

Elena stood with that same unhurried grace, waiting as Claire gathered her clutch. They navigated through the crowd, Elena somehow creating a path without seeming to part it, her body a gentle shield between Claire and the press of strangers. Claire felt hyperaware of her own movements—the way her dress clung to her hips, the careful placement of each step in her unfamiliar heels.

They settled into a curved booth tucked into a quiet alcove. The velvet was plush beneath Claire's fingers, and the lighting here was even softer, casting amber shadows across Elena's features. The booth created a small universe separate from the rest of the club, their knees almost touching beneath the low table.

"Better?" Elena asked, arranging her crimson skirt with a practiced gesture.

"I feel like I can breathe a little easier here," Claire admitted as she settled into the velvet booth. The fabric caressed her bare arms, surprisingly warm against her skin.

Elena smiled, the amber light catching the gold flecks in her brown eyes. "That's why I suggested it. The bar is for watching. These booths are for becoming."

Claire's eyebrows lifted. "Echo said something similar about drinks. First for arrival, second for becoming."

"Echo has a gift for seeing people at their crossroads." Elena leaned forward slightly, her crimson dress pooling like liquid around her. "So, Claire the graphic designer with the perfectly named cat—what made you choose this particular Friday night to visit The Glass Heel?"

The question hung between them, deceptively casual. Claire's fingers traced the edge of the table, buying time. The truth caught in her throat. Her fingers found a loose thread in the velvet booth, and she traced it, gathering her courage.

"I found it online," she said finally, her voice barely audible above the music. "A forum for... for people like me." The last words came out as a whisper.

Elena waited, her silence an invitation rather than a demand.

"This is my first night out," Claire continued, the words spilling out now. "As... as myself. As Claire."

She braced herself for the reaction—the widened eyes, the subtle recoil, the forced smile that never quite reached the eyes. But Elena's expression remained unchanged, her gaze steady and warm.

"Thank you for sharing that with me," Elena said simply. "That takes immense courage."

Claire exhaled, not realizing she'd been holding her breath. "You don't seem surprised."

"The Glass Heel welcomes many women on their first nights of authenticity," Elena said, her voice rich with understanding. "Including me, once upon a time."

Claire's head snapped up, her eyes widening.

"You're—"

"Yes," Elena nodded, a small smile playing at her lips. "Seven years ago, I stood outside these doors for nearly an hour. Terrified someone would see through me."

Claire felt something loosen in her chest, a knot of tension she hadn't realized was there. "How did you know you were ready?"

"I didn't," Elena said with a smile. "No one ever feels ready, Claire. I just reached a point where staying hidden hurt more than the risk of being seen."

Claire nodded, understanding washing over her. That tipping point between fear and necessity felt achingly familiar.

"My first night out was a disaster," Elena continued, leaning back against the velvet. "I wore six-inch heels I couldn't walk in and a dress so tight I couldn't breathe. I spent most of the night in the bathroom having a panic attack."

Claire's eyes widened. "Really? But you seem so... together."

Elena's laugh rolled through the air between them, rich and unrestrained. "Oh, honey. I was a mess. I knocked over three drinks, called the bartender 'sir' when she was clearly a woman, and when someone asked for my name, I forgot the one I'd chosen."

A small bubble of laughter escaped Claire's lips before she could stop it. The image of Elena—poised, elegant Elena—stumbling in too-high heels seemed impossible to reconcile with the woman sitting across from her.

"What name did you give instead?" Claire asked, curiosity warming her voice.

Elena leaned forward, eyes sparkling with mischief.

"My deadname? No. My high school nickname? No. I panicked and said 'Cher.' Just... Cher."

Claire's laughter burst free, genuine and surprised. "Like the singer?"

"Yes," Elena nodded, her smile brightening even further. "Though I sadly lacked the sequins and headdress to pull it off convincingly."

Claire's laughter came easier now, the sound surprising her with its freedom. Something was shifting between them, the air growing warmer, more permeable.

"I can't imagine you as anything other than..." she gestured vaguely at Elena's composed elegance.

"This?" Elena supplied. "Trust me, this took years of practice. And many, many embarrassing nights."

The confession wrapped around Claire like a blanket. Each word from Elena's lips chipped away at the wall Claire had built around herself. She found herself leaning forward, elbows on the table, the defensive hunch of her shoulders gradually relaxing.

"Did you always know?" The question slipped out before Claire could consider its weight.

"That I was a woman?" Elena took a sip of her drink, considering. "Yes and no. I knew something was fundamentally misaligned, but I didn't have the language for it until I was twenty-three."

Claire nodded, recognition flickering through her. "I used to think everyone felt like they were performing a role they hadn't auditioned for."

"Exactly. The terrible costume that never quite fits," Elena said. Her eyes held Claire's, reflecting understanding rather than pity. "When did you know?"

Claire's mouth went dry. When had she known? The question hung in the air between them, deceptively simple yet impossibly complex. Her fingers traced patterns in the condensation on her water glass as her mind raced through fragmented memories—playing with her mother's makeup at six, the crushing disappointment of puberty, the dreams where her body finally matched her soul.

"I'm not sure I do know," she admitted finally, her voice barely audible above the music. "Sometimes I wonder if this—" she gestured down at her emerald dress, her carefully applied makeup "—is really me or just... an act I'm putting on." The confession felt both terrifying and liberating, hanging in the air between them.

Elena's expression remained unchanged, no judgment shadowing her features. "The line between performance and authenticity is rarely clear for any woman. Cis women perform femininity too—we're just not asked to justify it."

Claire let the words settle over her. The thought was oddly comforting—that perhaps everyone was figuring it out as they went along, not just her.

The music shifted, the beat slowing to something rich and sultry. Elena's gaze drifted toward the dance floor, where couples were drawing closer together, bodies swaying in intimate synchronicity. When she looked back at Claire, there was a new warmth in her eyes.

"Would you like to dance?" Elena asked, extending her hand across the table.

Claire's heart lurched against her ribs. The booth had become a safe haven, and the thought of venturing onto the crowded dance floor sent a cold spike of panic through Claire's chest. She glanced down at her kitten heels, suddenly aware of how precarious they felt. The dance floor meant bodies in motion, eyes watching, judging. Her hand trembled slightly as she set her glass down.

"I'm not much of a dancer," she said, the excuse falling flat even to her own ears. How could she explain that dancing meant movement, and movement meant her body—this body that still sometimes felt like borrowed clothing—would be on display?

Elena's hand remained extended, patient as a promise. "Neither was I, once." Her eyes held Claire's, seeing past the excuse to the fear beneath. "The dance floor can feel like stepping into a spotlight."

Claire's throat tightened. How did Elena understand so precisely what she hadn't said?

"My hips don't..." Claire started, then stopped, swallowing hard. "I move wrong." The admission was barely audible, but in the intimate space of their booth, it hung between them like spun glass.

Elena's expression softened. "There's no wrong way to move, Claire. Only ways that haven't found their music yet." She leaned forward, her voice dropping to a confidential murmur. "When I first started dancing here, I was so focused on looking 'right' that I forgot to feel anything. I counted steps like math problems."

A small, surprised laugh escaped Claire's lips. "That's exactly what I'm afraid of doing," Claire admitted, a small smile tugging at the corners of her mouth. "Counting steps like I'm trying to solve an equation."

Elena's hand remained outstretched, an invitation hovering between them. In the amber light, her fingers looked strong yet gentle, capable of both leading and supporting.

"What if..." Claire began, her voice barely audible above the music. "What if I step on your toes? Or trip?"

"Then we'll laugh, and keep dancing," Elena replied simply. "The beauty of this place is that no one is watching as closely as you think."

Claire took a deep breath, feeling it expand her ribs against the silk of her dress. She thought of Echo's words: *Trust that feeling when it comes.* Before she could talk herself out of it, she placed her hand in Elena's.

"Okay," she whispered. "But don't say I didn't warn you."

Elena's smile was radiant as she rose from the booth, her crimson dress catching the light. She guided Claire to her feet with gentle pressure, her touch warm and steady. Claire wobbled slightly in her kitten heels, but Elena's hand at the small of her back steadied her immediately.

"I've got you," Elena murmured, close enough that Claire could feel her breath against her ear.

They moved toward the dance floor, weaving between tables and other patrons. Claire felt hyperaware of every step, of Elena's hand still resting at the small of her back. The press of bodies seemed to close in around them as they reached the edge of the dance floor, the music wrapping around them like a physical presence. Claire felt her breath quicken, her fingers tightening around Elena's.

"Just focus on me," Elena murmured, guiding Claire deeper into the crowd.

The dance floor opened before them, a sea of moving bodies bathed in amber and rose-gold light. Elena found them a small pocket of space near the center, turning to face Claire with those steady brown eyes. The music pulsed around them, a slow, sensual beat that seemed to vibrate through the soles of Claire's shoes.

Elena's hands settled at Claire's waist, light as butterflies but sure in their placement. The crimson silk of her dress whispered against Claire's fingers as she hesitantly placed her hands on Elena's shoulders. They stood like that for a moment, barely moving, as Claire's heart thundered in her chest.

"Close your eyes," Elena suggested, her voice a warm current against Claire's ear. "Just feel the music first."

Claire let her eyes flutter closed, surrendering to the

darkness behind her lids. The bass line throbbed beneath her feet, steady as a heartbeat. Elena's hands at her waist were gentle anchors, neither demanding nor directing—simply present.

"Now sway," Elena said softly. "Nothing complicated. Just your hips, following the beat."

Slowly, Claire's hips began to sway. The movement felt strange at first, disconnected from the rest of her body, but Elena matched her rhythm perfectly, their bodies finding a gentle synchronicity. The tension in Claire's shoulders began to dissolve as Elena guided her deeper into the music.

"That's it," Elena murmured, her voice barely audible above the sultry beat. "You're dancing."

Claire opened her eyes to find Elena's warm gaze on her, not evaluating, just present. Something about that look—acceptance without judgment—made Claire's movements loosen further. Elena's hands remained light on her waist, neither controlling nor demanding, simply supporting.

When the song shifted into something with a deeper bass, Elena moved imperceptibly closer. The heat of her body radiated through the thin silk of Claire's dress, warming her skin. Claire's breath caught as Elena's thumb traced a small circle against her waist, the gesture so subtle it might have been accidental.

"You're overthinking again," Elena said, a gentle smile playing at her lips. "I can see it in your eyes."

Claire exhaled a nervous laugh. "Is it that obvious?"

"Only to someone who's been there." Elena's hand slid to the small of Claire's back, guiding her into a gentle turn that somehow aligned perfectly with the music's flow. "Try something for me?"

Claire nodded, surprised by her own willingness to

trust.

"When you exhale, let your shoulders drop completely," Elena instructed.

Claire closed her eyes and exhaled deeply, letting her shoulders fall as Elena had instructed. Something shifted inside her as the tension drained from her body. The music swelled around them, no longer a mathematical problem to solve but a current carrying her forward.

Her hips found the rhythm without calculation, swaying in perfect counterpoint to Elena's movements. The emerald silk of her dress whispered against her thighs, no longer a costume but a second skin. Elena's hand pressed slightly firmer against the small of her back, and Claire leaned into the touch, surprising herself with how natural it felt.

"There you are," Elena murmured, her voice warm with approval.

The words bloomed inside Claire's chest. She opened her eyes to find Elena's gaze on her, rich with something that looked like recognition. Not of who she had been, but of who she was becoming in this moment.

The crowd around them blurred into insignificance. The dance floor was no longer a gauntlet to navigate but simply the space where their bodies conversed in a language older than words. Claire's awareness narrowed to the points where Elena touched her—the hand at her waist, fingers splayed against the silk; the gentle pressure guiding her through a turn; the whisper of breath against her temple when Elena leaned close.

When Elena guided her into a slow spin, Claire followed without hesitation, her body responding as if it had always known how to move this way. The emerald dress flared slightly with the movement, catching the amber light.

And in that moment, the crowd disappeared. The other dancers, the bar, the whole club—all of it faded into a warm, indistinct blur. There was only Elena, only the music, only the sensation of her own body moving with unexpected grace. Claire closed her eyes, surrendering to the rhythm that had somehow taken root inside her. Her mind quieted. The constant internal critic—the voice that had shadowed her every movement since childhood—fell silent.

Elena's hand slid to her hip, guiding her closer. Claire's body responded without hesitation, like water finding its natural course. The silk of her dress caressed her skin as she moved, each step feeling more natural than the last. Her arms lifted, no longer stiff with self-consciousness but flowing like ribbons in a gentle breeze.

Elena leaned in, her lips brushing the shell of Claire's ear. "You move like someone who's waited her whole life to be touched."

Claire's breath caught in her throat. The words slipped beneath her skin, touching something deep and unguarded. A shiver traveled down her spine, not from fear but from recognition—as if Elena had seen something in her that Claire herself had only glimpsed in dreams.

Something shifted inside her, a tectonic movement so profound she almost expected the floor to tremble beneath their feet. The feeling wasn't entirely new—more like a remembering, a return to a truth her body had always known but her mind had forgotten.

Chapter 3

Between the Beats

The music faded into the background as they returned to the sapphire booth, their bodies still humming with the memory of movement. Claire sank into the velvet cushions, her breath coming easier now, as if the dance had loosened something long-knotted inside her chest.

"Thank you," she whispered, her voice barely audible above the club's gentle pulse. "I never thought I could dance like that."

Elena settled beside her, closer than before, the crimson silk of her dress pooling against the emerald of Claire's. "You've always been able to. You just needed the right partner."

The world felt softer now, the edges of everything blurred into a gentle glow. Claire watched the amber light catch in Elena's dark curls, turning them almost bronze. The night had slipped into that magical hour when time seems to stretch, when strangers become confidants and truths rise to the surface like cream.

"Claire," Elena said, rolling the name on her tongue like tasting wine. "How long have you been Claire?"

The question settled between them, delicate but weighted. Claire's fingers traced the condensation on her water glass, drawing invisible patterns as she gathered her courage.

"Officially? Six months." She took a deep breath, the silk of her dress rising and falling with her chest. "But I've been Claire in my head for... forever, I think. Even before I knew that's who I was."

"Claire is a beautiful name," Elena said softly. "Did you choose it yourself?"

Claire nodded, her throat suddenly tight. The question was simple, but the answer felt like opening a door she'd kept locked for years.

"I found it in a book when I was twelve," she admitted, her voice barely above a whisper. "The main character was everything I wasn't – brave and sure of herself. I used to whisper it to myself at night, like a secret only I knew."

Elena's eyes never left her face, patient and attentive. The gentle encouragement in her gaze made Claire want to keep talking, to let the words spill out after years of careful containment.

"I tried other names first. Sarah. Jennifer. Elizabeth." Claire's fingers traced the rim of her glass. "But Claire was the only one that felt like coming home."

"It suits you," Elena said. "Clear. Luminous."

Claire felt heat rise to her cheeks. "Most days I don't feel either of those things."

"Who else knows you as Claire?" Elena asked, her

question gentle but direct.

Claire looked down at her hands, studying the careful polish on her nails – a pale pink she'd spent an hour applying and reapplying until each one was perfect.

"Almost no one," she confessed. "My therapist. A few people online. My cat." She attempted a laugh, but it caught in her throat. "Pathetic, right?"

"No," Elena said firmly, her voice warm with conviction. "It's not pathetic at all. It's brave."

Claire felt something tighten in her throat, a constellation of words she'd never spoken aloud forming there. The gentle acceptance in Elena's eyes made the world around them seem to recede further, until their booth felt like the only solid place in existence.

"Sometimes I feel like I'm living in two separate worlds," Claire said, her voice stronger now. "There's the world where I'm... the old me. Going through motions, nodding at the right times, saying things people expect. And then there's this hidden world where I'm Claire. Where I can breathe."

Elena reached across the table, her fingers hovering near Claire's but not quite touching, offering connection without demand.

"The isolation is the hardest part," Claire continued, surprised by her own candor. "Not just from other people, but from myself. Like I'm watching my own life through a window, never quite participating in it."

She took a sip of water, gathering courage from the simple act.

"There are days when I don't speak to anyone except Pixel. When I order delivery, I time it so I can just grab the bag without having to make eye contact. I work from home, I shop online, I..." She paused, embarrassed by the admission forming on her tongue. "I practice conversations in the mirror sometimes, just to hear a human voice."

The confession hung in the air between them. Claire waited for the look of pity she was sure would follow—the same expression her therapist wore whenever Claire mentioned her isolation. But Elena's eyes held only understanding, deep and genuine.

"I've never been kissed as Claire," she whispered, the words emerging before she could reconsider them. "I mean, I've been with people before, but... never as myself." She swallowed hard. "Sometimes I wonder if I ever will be. If anyone will ever see me as I am and still want to..."

The words trailed off, hanging in the air between them. Claire's heart hammered against her ribs, regret already forming. She'd said too much, revealed too much. But something about Elena's steady gaze made the vulnerability feel less like exposure and more like connection.

"Do you know what I see when I look at you, Claire?" Elena asked, her voice low and certain.

Claire shook her head, not trusting herself to speak.

"I see a woman who has fought her way into existence. Who chose her own name and claimed it, despite everything telling her she couldn't." Elena's fingers finally bridged the gap between them, brushing against Claire's with feather-light pressure. "There's a light in you that's all the more beautiful for having been hidden so long."

Claire felt heat rise to her cheeks, the gentle praise settling into places inside her that had been hollow for years. Elena's touch against her fingers was barely there, yet it anchored her to the moment with surprising strength.

Elena's eyes dropped to Claire's lips, lingering there

with such gentle attention that Claire felt her breath catch. The moment expanded between them, stretched and warm, filled with possibility. Elena shifted closer, the crimson silk of her dress whispering against the emerald of Claire's. The scent of her perfume—sandalwood and something darker—enveloped Claire like an embrace.

"Claire," Elena whispered, her voice barely audible above the music's pulse. "May I kiss you?"

The question hung in the air, delicate and profound. Claire felt her heart stutter, then race. She nodded, not trusting her voice to remain steady.

Elena's hand gracefully rose to cup her cheek, her thumb tenderly brushing the corner of her mouth with a precision that was both gentle and deliberate. She leaned forward with a languid slowness, each movement offering Claire a silent opportunity to pull away. Yet, retreat was the furthest thing from Claire's mind as Elena's lips finally made contact with hers.

The kiss wasn't an explosion of fireworks or a bolt of lightning. It was far more fundamental than that. It was like the first sip of cool, refreshing water after enduring a parched desert. Elena's lips were a soft whisper against hers, unhurried and gentle, like a calming tide. Claire felt herself melting into the embrace, her body responding to a truth her mind had only dared to dream of—this is what it means to be kissed as your true self.

The world around them faded away, narrowing to points of sensation: the warmth of Elena's palm caressing her cheek, the luxurious velvet booth a soft support beneath her fingers, the lingering taste of whiskey on Elena's lips that danced on her tongue. Claire felt a warmth unfurling within her, a forgotten heat reignited. Each gentle press of Elena's lips was an affirmation—yes, you are here; yes, you are real; yes, you are Claire.

When they finally parted, Claire's entire body

trembled with a newfound energy. A shiver cascaded through her, beginning at her lips and rippling outward until even her fingertips tingled with vibrant awareness. This wasn't the familiar tremor of anxiety or fear—this was recognition, a profound awakening, as if every cell in her body had suddenly become attuned to its own undeniable truth.

Elena's eyes searched her face, gentle and questioning. "Are you okay?"

"Yes," Claire whispered, surprised by the steadiness in her voice. "More than okay."

Elena smiled, tucking a strand of hair behind Claire's ear with tender precision. "Upstairs," she said softly, her voice low enough that only Claire could hear, "there are rooms. Private spaces where we could talk... or not talk. Where you could just be Claire, without having to guard yourself."

The invitation hung in the air between them, weighted with possibility. Claire felt her pulse quicken, not with fear but with a startling clarity of desire. The thought of being alone with Elena, of having space to unfold completely into herself without the weight of watching eyes—it pulled at something deep inside her.

"The rooms are beautiful," Elena continued, her thumb tracing small circles against Claire's palm. "Each one different. Echo designed them as sanctuaries. Places to discover parts of yourself you haven't met yet."

Claire's body shivered, a tremor that rippled through her core and out to her fingertips. It wasn't fear that caused this reaction—it was recognition. Recognition of a threshold about to be crossed, of a door opening to a room she'd always known existed but had never dared enter.

"The rooms upstairs," Elena continued, her voice a warm caress against Claire's ear, "they're designed for women like us. Places where masks can fall away completely." Her fingers traced a gentle path along Claire's wrist, leaving goosebumps in their wake. "Echo keeps a few keys for special guests. Women who need... sanctuary."

Claire's mouth went dry at the thought. A private room. Just her and Elena. No eyes watching, no performance necessary. Just the truth of who she was, laid bare before someone who might truly see her.

"Would you like that?" Elena asked, her question carrying no pressure, only possibility.

Claire looked into Elena's eyes, searching for any hint of insincerity or pity. She found neither—only a steady warmth that seemed to reach past her carefully constructed defenses.

"I want to go upstairs," Claire whispered, the words emerging with surprising conviction. They hung in the air between them, a declaration that felt both terrifying and inevitable.

Elena nodded, something like approval warming her gaze. But she didn't move, didn't rush. She simply waited, giving Claire space to be certain.

"I want to," Claire repeated herself, as if speaking the words again might somehow make them more real, more tangible. "I want to go upstairs with you."

Claire's words hung between them, a whispered confession that seemed to shift the air around them. Elena rose from the booth with that same fluid grace, extending a hand to help Claire to her feet. The touch felt different now—more certain, more electric—as if the kiss had opened a current between them that could no longer be contained.

"Are you sure?" Elena asked, her voice a warm breath against Claire's ear.

Claire nodded, not trusting her voice. Her body hummed with anticipation and something deeper—a bone-deep certainty that had been absent from her life for too long.

They moved through the club hand in hand, weaving between dancers whose swaying forms had blurred into mere shadows in Claire's heightened awareness. The music pounded around them, a rhythmic cacophony that seemed to echo from every corner, but Claire could only focus on her own heartbeat, a relentless drumbeat thundering in her ears like distant, powerful drums. Her kitten heels tapped against the glossy obsidian floor, each measured step growing more confident and assured than the one before, as if she were finding her own rhythm in the midst of the chaos.

The spiral staircase ascended majestically before them, entwined in intricate golden vines and ornate wrought iron, leading to mysteries Claire had only glimpsed in the most secretive corners of her dreams. The staircase spiraled upwards, disappearing into the shadows where secrets whispered and beckoned. At its base stood Echo, statuesque and exuding an air of ancient wisdom, as though she had been waiting for precisely this moment to unfold.

In her slender palm rested a single key, its brass surface gleaming with a warm, amber glow that seemed to pulse with the promise of hidden wonders. Etched into its surface was a delicate rose, each petal rendered with exquisite precision and care, as if a master artist had spent a lifetime perfecting its beauty. Echo's eyes, deep and knowing, met Claire's with an intensity that spoke of shared secrets and untold stories, a playful smile dancing at the corners of her crimson lips, hinting at the adventures that awaited.

Claire reached out, her fingers trembling slightly as they closed around the cool, smooth metal. The weight of it surprised her—heavier than it appeared, as if it carried more than just the promise of a door unlocked, perhaps a world of possibilities. Echo's fingers brushed softly against hers as she released the key, the brief contact feeling like a blessing, a gentle affirmation.

As they ascended the grand, spiraling staircase, Claire felt the weight of the evening fall away like a discarded cloak. Each step carried her higher, away from the woman she had been when she entered The Glass Heel, toward someone new—someone who had danced freely without counting steps, who had been kissed and trembled with recognition rather than fear, embracing the moment.

Elena's hand remained intertwined with hers, a steady anchor in this vast sea of transformation. The staircase curved elegantly, revealing a hallway lined with doors, each one distinct and inviting—some crafted from dark wood intricately carved with swirling patterns, others painted in rich, alluring colors that seemed to shimmer and dance in the dim, ambient light.

"Which one?" Claire whispered, the key warm now in her palm.

"The one with the rose," Elena murmured, guiding Claire's attention to a door at the far end of the hallway. "The key will tell us."

They ascended the spiral staircase together, the wrought iron cool beneath Claire's fingertips as she steadied herself. Each step carried her further from the pulsing heart of the club below, the music gradually fading until it became just a distant heartbeat. The air changed as they climbed—warmer, more intimate, carrying subtle notes of sandalwood and amber that seemed to wrap around Claire like an embrace.

At the top of the stairs, the hallway opened before them, bathed in a gentle amber glow that made the walls themselves appear to breathe. Claire paused, taken aback by the unexpected beauty of this hidden corridor. Unlike the sensual darkness of the club below, the hallway was illuminated by antique sconces that cast pools of golden light at regular intervals, their flames dancing behind amber glass.

Between each sconce hung photographs—dozens of them—their frames varying from ornate gilt to simple black, creating a timeline that stretched the length of the hallway. Claire's steps slowed as her eyes caught on the images. Women's faces looked back at her from different eras—some in sepia tones with high collars and stern expressions, others in vibrant color with bold makeup and defiant smiles. Their eyes seemed to follow her, not in judgment but in recognition.

"The history of The Glass Heel," Elena explained softly, her voice barely disturbing the hallway's hushed atmosphere. "Every woman who found herself here."

Claire stopped before a photograph from what looked like the 1920s—a group of women in beaded dresses with short, bobbed hair, arms around each other's waists, their expressions a mixture of joy and conspiracy. Something about their eyes, their closeness, made Claire's throat tighten.

"Were they...?" she began, not quite able to form the question.

"Like us?" Elena finished, her thumb brushing gently across Claire's knuckles. "Some of them, yes. Others were seeking different freedoms. The Glass Heel has always been a sanctuary for women who didn't fit the world outside."

Claire moved slowly down the hallway, drawn from one photograph to the next. The wooden floorboards creaked softly beneath her heels, the sound somehow comforting in its solidity. The walls themselves seemed to hold memories—not just in the photographs, but in the very plaster and paint, as if decades of whispered confessions and newfound courage had seeped into the building's bones.

A photograph from the 1950s caught her eye—a woman in a tailored suit, her short hair slicked back, looking directly at the camera with a challenging gaze. Beside her stood another woman in a full-skirted dress, their hands barely touching at the edges of the frame. The intimacy of that small contact made Claire's chest ache.

"Did they find happiness?" she asked, her voice soft in the hushed corridor.

Elena's eyes lingered on the photograph. "Some did. Some didn't. But they all found truth here."

Claire continued down the hallway, each step bringing her closer to the door at the end. The photos became more recent as they progressed—colors brightening, hairstyles evolving, yet the same searching look remained in the women's eyes. A sisterhood spanning decades, all seeking the same elusive freedom.

The floorboards whispered beneath her heels, their age speaking through gentle creaks that seemed to echo the sighs of countless women who had walked this path before her. The scent of aged wood and beeswax polish mingled with Elena's perfume, creating an atmosphere that felt both sacred and intimate. Claire's fingers tightened around the key, its weight now familiar in her palm.

"The rooms change," Elena said, her voice barely above a whisper. "Echo says they become what each woman needs most."

Claire looked at her, questions forming on her lips, but Elena simply smiled—that same patient, knowing smile that had drawn Claire to her on the dance floor.

They reached the end of the hallway where a single door stood. Unlike the others they had passed, this one was painted a deep, velvety crimson with a brass doorknob worn smooth by countless hands. In its center, carved with exquisite detail, was a rose in full bloom—its petals unfurling with such lifelike precision that Claire could almost imagine its perfume. The carved pattern matched the one on her key exactly.

Claire paused before it, suddenly aware of her heartbeat, a wild rhythm that seemed to fill the hushed corridor. The weight of the key in her palm felt significant now, like a talisman entrusted to her safekeeping. Elena stood close beside her, her presence a warm certainty in the quiet hallway.

"This is it," Claire whispered, her voice barely disturbing the reverent silence.

She lifted the key, noticing how her hand trembled slightly. The brass caught the amber light from the sconces, reflecting it in golden fragments across her skin. For a moment, she hesitated, aware of standing on a threshold that, once crossed, could never be uncrossed. Elena's hand settled at the small of her back, neither pushing nor pulling—simply present, a gentle affirmation.

Claire slid the key into the lock. It fit perfectly, as if made for her hand alone. The mechanism turned with a smooth, well-oiled click that resonated through her fingers and up her arm. The sound seemed to echo in the hushed hallway, marking a moment of irreversible change.

As she turned the key, Claire felt a subtle shift within herself—something unlocking that mirrored the door's mechanism. The faces in the photographs along the hall seemed to watch with gentle approval, witnesses to a ritual they themselves had once performed. The door to the Rose Room eased open slightly, releasing a breath of warm air that carried hints of rose petals and warm amber. Claire held her breath, the moment suspended between what was and what might be.

Chapter 4

The Room Above the Music

The door opened to a world of golden light and whispered promises.

Claire stepped inside, her breath catching at the vision before her. The Rose Room enveloped her in warmth that seemed to radiate from the very walls. Amber light suffused everything—not the harsh glare of electricity, but the living glow of dozens of candles placed in crystal holders throughout the space, their flames dancing in perfect stillness.

The scent hit her next—lavender layered over something deeper, something that reminded her of summer evenings and secret gardens. It filled her lungs, loosening something that had been tight inside her chest for as long as she could remember.

"It's beautiful," she whispered, the words barely disturbing the room's hushed atmosphere.

Elena closed the door behind them with a soft, deliberate click, a sound that seemed to seal them away from the bustling world outside. The cozy warmth of the room enveloped them, contrasting sharply with the chill they left behind. Claire listened intently as the lock turned with a quiet, metallic whisper, a sound that was both thrilling in its promise of privacy and terrifying in its sense of irrevocable finality. The air inside was thick with anticipation, as if the very walls held their breath in suspense.

The room unfurled before her like a dream made tangible, each detail more enchanting than the last. A massive, sprawling bed dominated the center, its ornate frame carved with intricate patterns that whispered of elegance and time. The linens draped over it were the color of cream and rose petals, soft and inviting, while the pillows were arranged in a sumptuous display, beckoning her to sink into their comforting embrace and drift into oblivion. To her right, a copper bathtub stood resplendent in the gentle glow of flickering candlelight, its surface polished to a mirror-like sheen. It was deep enough to offer complete submersion, a sanctuary of warmth and relaxation, adorned with brass fixtures that caught the light in shimmering, golden flickers. Steam rose languidly from its surface, curling in the air and carrying with it a heady scent of rose oil mixed with an elusive fragrance Claire couldn't quite name—something that smelled like adventure, like untapped potential, like pure, unbridled possibility.

"How did they know?" Claire asked, turning to face Elena.

"Echo," Elena answered simply, the name carrying both explanation and reverence. "She has a gift for knowing what each woman needs when she arrives."

The hotel room embraced Claire like a physical manifestation of tenderness. Soft rose-colored light bathed every surface, glowing from the candles and casting gentle shadows that danced across Elena's face. The lavender scent mingled with the rose oil from the bath, creating an atmosphere that seemed designed to lower defenses and invite vulnerability.

Claire moved further into the room, her fingers trailing across a velvet chaise positioned near tall windows draped with gauzy curtains. Everything felt deliberately chosen—the plush carpet beneath her kitten heels, the artful arrangement of fresh flowers on the bedside table, the absence of mirrors except for one small oval near the bath. This was a space built not for critique or performance, but for gentle acceptance.

Elena moved toward the center of the room, her silhouette outlined by candlelight. Without speaking, she reached for the clasp at her neck, unfastening the single hook that held her crimson dress in place. The fabric loosened, sliding over her shoulders with deliberate slowness. She maintained eye contact with Claire as the silk cascaded down her body, pooling at her feet like spilled wine.

Claire's breath caught in her throat. Elena stood before her in nothing but a black lace bralette and matching underwear, her bronze skin glowing in the amber light. There was no hesitation in her posture, no attempt to cover or hide—just the quiet confidence of a woman entirely at home in her body.

"You're staring," Elena said, her voice warm with amusement.

"You're beautiful," Claire whispered, the words escaping before she could trap them.

Elena stepped out of the circle of crimson silk, moving toward Claire with unhurried grace. Her fingers brushed Claire's cheek, trailing down to rest at the neckline of her emerald dress.

"May I?" she asked, her voice soft but clear in the candlelit room.

Claire nodded, unable to form words as her heart hammered against her ribs. Elena's fingers found the zipper at the back of her dress, drawing it down with gentle precision. The sound of it—that quiet, metallic whisper—seemed to fill the entire room.

The emerald silk slipped from Claire's shoulders. Elena's fingers glided along the curve of Claire's shoulders as the fabric fell, exposing pale skin that shimmered with a golden hue in the candlelight. Claire shivered, not from the chill, but from the tender reverence in Elena's touch.

"You're trembling," Elena whispered, her breath warm against Claire's ear.

"I'm not used to being seen," Claire admitted, fighting the urge to cross her arms over her chest. The simple cotton bra she wore suddenly seemed inadequate compared to Elena's lace, but Elena's eyes held no judgment—only appreciation.

With careful movements, Elena guided the dress down Claire's arms, her fingertips leaving trails of warmth on Claire's skin. The silk slipped over Claire's hips and joined Elena's crimson pool on the floor. Claire stood in her underwear, her heart thundering so loudly she was certain Elena could hear it.

"Beautiful," Elena murmured, stepping back slightly as if to better appreciate the sight before her. Her gaze traveled over Claire's body with such tenderness that Claire felt herself flush from her chest to her hairline.

Elena's hands returned to Claire's shoulders, tracing down her arms with feather-light touches. Each caress was deliberate, unhurried, as if Elena were memorizing the texture of her skin. Claire closed her eyes, surrendering to the sensation of being touched with such care.

"May I?" Elena asked again, her fingers finding the clasp of Claire's bra.

Claire nodded. The world narrowed to a single point of contact—Elena's fingertips against the clasp of her bra. A whisper of pressure, then release. The cotton loosened around her ribcage, suddenly weightless. Elena's hands traced the straps downward, each inch of revealed skin tingling in the wake of her touch until the garment surrendered completely, drifting to rest atop the abandoned dresses below.

"You're shaking," Elena whispered, her hands hovering just above Claire's skin, radiating warmth without touching.

"I'm scared," Claire admitted, her voice barely audible even in the hushed room. "Not of you. Of being... seen. Really seen."

Elena nodded, understanding filling her eyes. "Close your eyes if it helps."

Claire let her eyelids flutter closed, darkness enveloping her as Elena's hands finally made contact with her bare shoulders. The touch was featherlight, fingertips tracing the contours of her collarbone with unhurried appreciation. Each caress felt like a benediction, a silent affirmation of her body exactly as it was.

Elena's hands moved down her arms, across her ribs, mapping the landscape of her skin with tender curiosity. There was no rush in her exploration, no demand or expectation—just a gentle acknowledgment of each curve and hollow. Claire kept her eyes closed, allowing herself to experience the pure sensation of being touched with such care, such attention.

"You're holding your breath," Elena murmured, her lips close to Claire's ear. "Breathe with me."

Claire exhaled slowly, letting the rhythm of Elena's

breathing guide her own. The air left her lungs in a gentle stream, carrying away tension she hadn't realized she'd been holding.

"That's it," Elena murmured, her voice a caress against Claire's ear.

Elena's fingers traced a path down Claire's sides, each touch deliberate and unhurried. She moved with reverent patience, as if unwrapping a gift meant to be savored rather than rushed. When her hands reached Claire's hips, they paused at the elastic band of her cotton underwear.

"Is this okay?" Elena asked, her voice soft but clear in the candlelit room.

Claire nodded, then finding her voice, whispered, "Yes."

Elena knelt before her, a priestess at worship. Her fingers hooked gently into the cotton, easing it down with such care that Claire barely felt the fabric sliding against her skin. The underwear joined the growing constellation of discarded clothing on the floor. Elena remained kneeling, her eyes traveling up Claire's body with undisguised appreciation.

"Look at me," Elena said.

Claire opened her eyes, vulnerable and exposed in the golden light. She expected to feel shame or the desperate urge to cover herself, but Elena's gaze held such tender admiration that Claire felt something else entirely—a strange, new pride in her own skin.

"There you are," Elena whispered, rising slowly to her feet. "All of you."

"Claire." Elena reached for her hand, drawing her toward the bed. "What do you want tonight?"

The question hung in the air, simple yet profound. Claire felt her throat tighten as she considered how to answer. What did she want? The possibilities seemed endless, overwhelming.

"I don't know," she whispered. "I just want to feel... real."

Elena nodded as if this made perfect sense. "Then let's start there."

She guided Claire to the edge of the bed, its plush surface giving way beneath her weight. The sheets were cool against her bare skin, a whisper of sensation that heightened her awareness of her nakedness. Elena stood before her, still in her black lace underwear, her body a sculpture of shadows and golden light.

"May I join you?" Elena asked, her voice soft in the candlelit room.

Claire nodded, her heart fluttering against her ribs like a trapped bird. Elena reached behind her back, unfastening her bra with practiced ease. The lace fell away, revealing the gentle curve of her breasts. She slipped out of her underwear next, the movement fluid and without self-consciousness. Claire couldn't help but stare, taking in the beauty of Elena's body—the soft swell of her hips, the flat plane of her stomach, the graceful length of her legs.

"You're staring again," Elena said, a smile warming her voice.

"I can't help it," Claire admitted. "You're... perfect."

"I'm not," Elena said softly, joining Claire on the bed. "Nobody is."

She settled beside Claire, their bodies not quite touching. The mattress dipped slightly under their combined weight, creating a gentle gravity that drew them toward each other. Claire could feel the warmth radiating from Elena's skin, could smell the subtle perfume that clung to her—sandalwood and something darker, more intimate.

"What happens now?" Claire whispered, her voice catching on the last word.

Elena smiled, her eyes crinkling at the corners. "Whatever we want. There's no script, no expectations." She reached out, her fingertips barely grazing Claire's cheek. "We explore. We discover. We simply... be."

Claire leaned into the touch, a shiver running through her as Elena's fingers made contact with her skin. The warmth of Elena's fingers sent a delightful tingling sensation coursing through her, igniting every nerve they brushed against. The gentle caress meandered down her jawline, tracing the elegant curve with a feather-light touch, then continued its journey along the smooth column of her throat. Goosebumps blossomed in its wake, a testament to the electric connection between them. Elena's touch was light yet purposeful, as if she were deciphering a hidden code etched into Claire's skin, learning its secret language with each tender stroke.

"May I touch you?" Elena asked, her hand hovering over Claire's collarbone.

Claire nodded, her breath shallow in her chest. "Yes."

Elena's palm settled against Claire's skin, warm and assured, like the sun's gentle kiss at dawn. She traced the elegant curve of Claire's shoulder with a delicate, deliberate touch, journeying down the length of her arm with a tenderness that spoke volumes. Her fingers lingered around Claire's wrist, circling it with a feather-light caress before gracefully retracing their path back up. Each touch was unhurried, brimming with appreciation, as though Elena were uncovering a hidden treasure with every inch of Claire's skin.

Elena's hand then journeyed to Claire's sternum, lingering there with a deep reverence as if seeking to absorb the rhythmic dance of her heartbeat beneath the surface. The warmth of her palm spread like a soothing balm through Claire's chest, infusing her very bones with a profound sense of connection and a gentle serenity that enveloped her like a comforting embrace.

"Tell me what feels good," Elena whispered, her eyes never leaving Claire's face. "Your pleasure matters here."

Claire swallowed hard, unused to being asked what she wanted. "I like... I like the way you're touching me now. Like I'm something precious."

A smile bloomed across Elena's face. "You are precious." Her hand drifted lower, tracing the gentle curve of Claire's breast. "Every inch of you deserves attention."

The gentle touch sent shivers cascading like a frosty waterfall through Claire's body. She gasped, a sharp intake of breath that echoed in the quiet room, as Elena's thumb brushed delicately across her nipple. The sensation was so exquisite, so electrifying, that it teetered on the edge of overwhelming. Elena paused, her eyes locked onto Claire's face, watching with careful attention as a symphony of emotions played across it.

"Too much?" she asked.

Claire shook her head. "No. It's just... intense. In a good way."

Elena nodded, resuming her gentle exploration with a quiet reverence. Her fingers traced the delicate contours of Claire's body with unhurried curiosity, detailing every subtle rise and fall. She lingered on the graceful slope of her ribs, where each bone seemed to hold its own secret rhythm. Her touch glided over the soft swell of Claire's stomach, as if caressing the surface of a serene pond. She continued to the curve of her hip, a smooth arc that spoke of elegance and strength. Each touch was deliberate and tender, an expression of pure appreciation, entirely free from judgment or demand.

"You can touch me too," Elena murmured, taking

Claire's hand and guiding it to her shoulder. "If you want to."

Claire's fingers appeared almost ghostly white against the rich, sun-kissed hue of Elena's tanned skin, the sharp contrast between them both captivating and vivid. Elena's shoulder was a symphony of smoothness and strength, its surface sleek and taut, revealing a faint yet defined outline of muscles that hinted at her athletic prowess. As Claire gently traced her fingers down the length of Elena's arm, she observed the intricate network of delicate veins weaving just beneath the surface, like fragile blue-green threads under the golden canvas of her skin.

"That's it," Elena whispered. "There's no right or wrong way to touch. Just what feels good."

Claire's boldness grew with every passing second, her palm pressing firmly against the smooth expanse of Elena's collarbone, the warmth of her skin and the strong, steady pulse beneath it electrifying her touch. She followed the elegant, graceful curve of Elena's throat, her fingers dancing lightly along the delicate skin, tracing a path down to the tender hollow where her collarbones converged. Elena's eyes fluttered closed, her eyelashes casting soft shadows on her cheeks, and her lips parted slightly in a silent invitation as Claire's exploration continued, each touch charged with unspoken emotion.

"Is this okay?" Claire asked, her voice barely audible in the candlelit room.

"More than okay," Elena murmured, her breath catching as Claire's fingertips brushed the swell of her breast.

They moved together like dancers learning a new choreography, each touch a question, each sigh an answer. Elena's hand gently found Claire's waist, drawing her closer until their bodies pressed together, skin to skin, like a seamless fabric. The contact sent a ripple of sensation through Claire—an enveloping warmth, a velvety softness, the gentle, tender press of Elena's breasts against her own, creating an intimate symphony of connection.

Claire gasped, her breath catching at the intimacy of it, at how perfectly right it felt to be held in this way. Elena's lips, soft and inviting, found her neck, pressing delicate, lingering kisses against her pulse point, as if writing a love letter onto her skin. Each kiss was gentle, unhurried, like the slow unfolding of a flower in the morning sun, as if they had all the time in the world to discover the depths of each other.

Claire closed her eyes, surrendering completely to the waves of sensation that coursed through her. This wasn't like anything she'd experienced before—there was no script to follow, no performance to give, no expectations other than to be entirely present in her own body. Elena's mouth traveled slowly down her neck, each movement deliberate and tender, pausing at the hollow of her throat where her pulse fluttered like a captured bird, wild and free.

"You taste like lavender," Elena murmured against her skin. "And something uniquely you."

A soft moan escaped Claire's lips as Elena's mouth continued its journey, trailing kisses across her collarbone. Each touch was deliberate, attentive—as if Elena was memorizing the landscape of her body through taste and texture. Claire's hands found Elena's hair, fingers tangling in the dark curls, not to guide but simply to anchor herself in the moment.

Elena's palm skimmed down Claire's side, following the gentle curve of her waist to her hip. The touch was questioning, patient. When she reached the sensitive skin of Claire's inner thigh, she paused, looking up to meet Claire's gaze.

"Is this okay?" she asked, her voice husky but clear.

"Yes," Claire whispered, the word more breath than sound.

Elena's fingers danced gracefully across her bare thigh, tracing intricate patterns that spiraled upward with exquisite slowness. Each gentle circle drew closer to where Claire's body was beginning to respond, her penis stirring against her inner thigh. Claire's breath hitched as she felt herself hardening under Elena's gaze—their nakedness suddenly more real, more vulnerable than moments before. Her pulse quickened as Elena's eyes briefly followed the path of her own hand, then returned to Claire's face with undiminished warmth. A flush spread like wildfire up Claire's neck and cheeks as she fought the instinct to cover herself, to hide this most honest physical reaction to Elena's soft, teasing touch.

"I—I'm sorry," she whispered, the words tumbling out before she could stop them. Her hands moved instinctively to cover herself.

Elena caught her wrists gently, her touch feather-light. "Claire, look at me."

Claire raised her eyes slowly, terrified of what she might see—disgust, disappointment, rejection. Instead, Elena's gaze held nothing but warmth.

"There's nothing to apologize for," Elena said softly. "Your body is responding exactly as it should to pleasure. That's beautiful."

The knot in Claire's chest loosened slightly. "But I thought you might not want—"

"I want you," Elena interrupted, her voice low and certain. "All of you. Exactly as you are."

She leaned forward, pressing her lips to Claire's in a kiss that felt like a promise. When she pulled back, her eyes were dark with desire. "May I show you?"

Claire nodded, not trusting her voice.

Elena's hand returned to her inner thigh, her touch slow and deliberate. There was no hesitation in her movements, no hint of reluctance—only a deep appreciation that made Claire's skin tingle wherever she touched.

"Tell me what feels good," Elena murmured against her ear. "What do you want?"

The question hovered between them, delicate as the candlelight dancing across their skin. Claire felt the words catch in her throat—how could she possibly articulate desires she'd barely acknowledged to herself? Her entire body hummed with sensation, every nerve ending alive with a sensitivity she'd never experienced before.

"I want..." she began, the words barely audible. "I want to feel... real. With you."

Elena's smile was understanding, patient. "Then let's discover that together."

Her touch was feather-light as she traced a path up Claire's inner thigh, each circle bringing her fingers closer to where Claire's body pulsed with need. When her hand finally made contact, Claire gasped, her hips lifting slightly off the bed. Elena's touch was knowing yet exploratory, as if learning the unique landscape of Claire's pleasure for the first time.

"Like this?" Elena whispered, her fingers finding a rhythm that made Claire's breath catch.

"Yes," Claire breathed, her eyes fluttering closed as waves of sensation washed through her. "Just like that."

Elena maintained her tender care, observing Claire's expression with clear admiration. Her actions were unhurried, focused solely on enjoying the present. Claire found herself yielding to the feeling, her body reacting with a sincerity that both scared and excited her.

Elena's lips grazed Claire's abdomen, leaving a path of

gentle kisses that slowly moved downward. Her hands softly opened Claire's thighs, making room for herself between them. She glanced up, her eyes connecting with Claire's, softly asking a question.

"May I?" she asked, her breath warm against Claire's sensitive skin.

Claire nodded, unable to form words as her heart hammered wildly. The sight of Elena between her legs, looking up with such tender desire, was almost too much to bear. And then Elena lowered her head, and the warm wetness of her mouth enveloped Claire.

The sensation tore a gasp from Claire's throat. Her back arched involuntarily, her fingers clutching at the sheets beneath her. Elena's touch was gentle, exploratory—her tongue tracing patterns that sent electricity coursing through Claire's body. Each stroke was deliberate, as if Elena were learning a new language through touch alone.

"Oh," Claire breathed, the word more sound than speech as Elena found a particularly sensitive spot. Her hips rose slightly, seeking more of that exquisite pressure.

Elena responded to the unspoken request, focusing her attention there with delicate precision. Her hands settled on Claire's hips, steadying her as she continued her gentle exploration. There was no rush to her movements, no goal beyond discovering what brought Claire the most pleasure.

Claire's eyes fluttered closed, surrendering to the pure sensation of being touched with such care. The world narrowed to points of contact—a warm mouth, a gentle tongue, fingers steadying her hips. Claire whimpered as Elena's lips enveloped her completely, the sensation unlike anything she'd experienced before. This wasn't clinical or performative—this was worship, tender and reverent.

Elena moved with deliberate slowness, her tongue

exploring, learning what made Claire's breath catch and her hips rise from the bed. Each time Claire responded with a gasp or a trembling sigh, Elena would linger there, her attention focused entirely on that spot until Claire was quivering beneath her touch.

"Elena," Claire whispered, her voice breaking on the name. Her fingers tangled in Elena's dark curls, not guiding, just connecting, needing an anchor as pleasure built within her.

Elena hummed in response, the vibration sending new ripples of sensation through Claire's body. She continued her gentle exploration, her tongue finding a rhythm that made Claire's thighs tense and her breath come in short, desperate gasps.

There was no rush to Elena's movements, no goal beyond Claire's pleasure. She took her time, attentive to each response, each subtle shift of Claire's hips. When she found a particularly sensitive spot, she focused there with tender precision, her movements becoming more deliberate.

Claire felt herself building toward something immense, something that both terrified and beckoned her. Her body tensed, hovering on the edge of release. Elena sensed the change, her movements becoming more focused, more certain.

"I can't—" Claire gasped, the words dissolving into a strangled cry as the pleasure crested, washing through her in waves that seemed to reach every cell of her body. Her back arched off the bed, her fingers clutching desperately at the sheets.

The intensity of it stole her breath, her vision blurring as tears sprang unbidden to her eyes. One escaped, tracking a warm path down her temple and into her hair. The release wasn't just physical—it felt as though something deep inside her had broken open, exposing a raw, vulnerable part of herself she'd kept hidden for so long.

Elena moved up her body with fluid grace, gathering Claire into her arms as the aftershocks rippled through her. She brushed the tear away with her thumb, her touch impossibly gentle.

"You're crying," Elena whispered, her palm warm against Claire's cheek.

Claire nodded, unable to speak as emotion continued to surge through her. The tenderness in Elena's eyes was almost too much to bear.

Elena cupped her face between both hands, her gaze steady and certain. "You're not broken. You're just new."

The words settled into Claire like stones dropping into still water, sending ripples of recognition through her. New. Not wrong, not broken, not pretending—just at the beginning of something. The simplicity of it made her breath catch.

"How did you know that's what I needed to hear?" Claire whispered, her voice rough with emotion.

Elena's smile was warm with understanding. "Because I've been where you are," she said softly. "I remember what it was like to discover myself for the first time."

Claire felt the weight of the day settling into her bones, a pleasant heaviness that made her eyelids droop. The emotional release had left her drained yet somehow lighter, as if something long-carried had finally been set down. Elena seemed to sense her exhaustion, drawing her closer until Claire's head rested against her shoulder.

"Rest," Elena whispered, her fingers tracing gentle patterns along Claire's spine. "You're safe here."

Claire nestled against Elena's warmth, her body fitting perfectly into the gentle curves and comforting hollows of

Elena's form, like pieces of a puzzle coming together. The candles flickered softly around them, their golden light dancing across the bed and casting shadows that swayed with the flames. Elena pulled the soft, silken sheets over their entwined bodies, cocooning them in a soothing embrace. The air was rich with the scent of lavender, a fragrant spell that wrapped around them protectively, calming every anxious thought.

Elena's heartbeat pulsed steady and strong beneath Claire's ear, a rhythmic lullaby that slowed as sleep approached, like a gentle tide receding. Claire's own pulse gradually synchronized with it, their bodies finding a serene harmony in this most fundamental of life's dances. Her breathing deepened, rising and falling in perfect sync with Elena's, a timeless dance of breath shared between two souls.

The world beyond the Rose Room faded into oblivion, disappearing into the night. There was only this—this perfect cocoon of warmth and acceptance, this exquisite moment of being exactly who she was meant to be. Claire's last conscious thought, as sleep tenderly claimed her, was that she had never felt so completely at home in her own skin, enveloped in a sense of belonging that was as profound as it was peaceful.

Chapter 5

In the Morning Light

Claire woke to light—golden, weightless, filtering through gauze curtains like something from a dream. For a moment, she floated in that liminal space between sleeping and waking, her body heavy with contentment, her mind unmoored from the persistent anxieties that usually greeted her mornings.

The unfamiliar softness beneath her registered first. Not her worn cotton sheets, but something silken that caressed her bare skin. Then the warmth beside her—a living, breathing warmth that rose and fell with gentle rhythm.

Elena.

The name bloomed in Claire's mind as memory returned in a rush. The Glass Heel. The dance floor. The spiral staircase and the room with the rose-carved door. Elena's hands, her mouth, her whispered words. Claire felt heat rise to her cheeks as fragments of the night reassembled themselves—not with shame, but with a startled wonder.

She turned her head gingerly on the plush pillow, cautious not to disturb the serene presence of the woman slumbering beside her. Elena lay gracefully on her side, one arm nestled beneath her pillow, the other delicately draped in the narrow space that separated them. In the gentle embrace of sleep, her features appeared softer, more vulnerable, the composed mask of daytime confidence gently unraveled by the tender threads of dreams. Her dark, silken lashes brushed lightly against her cheeks, and her lips, slightly parted, released a series of soft, rhythmic exhalations that whispered into the quiet room.

Claire gazed at her with a reverence so profound it resembled a silent prayer. The elegant curve of Elena's neck was like a sculpture crafted by a master artist, while the soft shadow of her collarbone added depth to the scene. The gentle rise and fall of the sheet draped across her bare shoulder created a rhythm that matched the serenity of the moment. Morning light streamed through the window, capturing in its glow Elena's dark curls, which cascaded across the pillow like a waterfall of silk, their edges shimmering with a bronze hue.

Claire's gaze shifted past Elena to the wall beyond, where a mirror hung in an ornate frame. From this angle, she could see both of them reflected there—Elena in peaceful slumber, and herself, wide-eyed and tousled from sleep.

The sight of her own reflection made her breath catch in her throat like a startled bird. Was that really her? This woman with cheeks flushed the delicate pink of dawn-touched clouds, eyes liquid and luminous as forest pools after rain, her chestnut hair tumbled across the ivory pillowcase in waves that caught the light like burnished copper pennies? She looked... different. Not physically transformed—the small scar at her temple remained, the slight asymmetry of her eyebrows hadn't changed overnight—but something profound had shifted in how she inhabited her skin, as if she'd finally settled into a house she'd been rattling around in for years.

Claire eased herself up onto one elbow, careful not to disturb Elena's sleep. She studied her reflection more carefully now. The mirror captured her bare shoulders, the gentle slope where they met her neck, the hollow of her throat where her pulse beat steady and strong. Her lips were slightly swollen from Elena's kisses, her skin bearing the faintest marks where Elena's mouth had traveled.

But it was her eyes that truly captivated her attention—clear and unwavering, meeting their own reflection without a hint of hesitation. Gone was the familiar shadow of apology that had haunted them for so long, like an overcast sky finally giving way to sunlight.

This was her. Not some version she was striving to become, nor a performance of femininity she was attempting to perfect—just Claire, precisely as she was. The woman in the mirror looked... serene. Grounded. As if she'd finally arrived at a place she was meant to be, a sanctuary where she belonged.

A gentle movement beside her pulled Claire's focus back to Elena. The dark-haired woman stirred delicately, her eyelashes fluttering like the wings of a resting butterfly against her cheeks before they lifted to reveal those warm brown eyes, now softened by the embrace of sleep.

"Good morning," Elena murmured, her voice husky from disuse.

"Morning," Claire replied, suddenly shy despite their intimacy the night before. She tugged the sheet higher, covering herself to the collarbone.

Elena noticed the gesture and smiled gently. "Last night wasn't a dream, then?" she asked, stretching languorously beneath the sheets.

"No," Claire whispered. "It wasn't a dream."

Elena propped herself up on one elbow, mirroring Claire's position. Her dark curls tumbled around her shoulders, catching the golden morning light. "How do you feel?"

The question was simple but profound. Claire considered it carefully, taking inventory of her body, her emotions.

"I feel... present," she said finally. "Like I'm actually here, in my skin, instead of watching myself from somewhere else."

Elena's smile deepened, crinkling the corners of her eyes. "That's a beautiful way to put it."

She reached out, her fingers tracing a gentle pattern on Claire's arm. The simple touch sent warmth radiating through Claire's body, as natural as sunlight on skin.

"Did you sleep well?" Elena asked, her voice still carrying that morning softness, like velvet wrapped around each word.

Claire nodded. "Better than I have in... I can't remember how long." She hesitated, then admitted, "I usually have trouble sleeping. My mind races."

"And last night?"

"Quiet," Claire said. "Everything was quiet."

Elena's smile deepened, her eyes crinkling at the corners in a way that made Claire's heart flutter. There was something so intimate about seeing someone's morning face—the slight puffiness around the eyes, the faint crease from the pillow marking her cheek, the natural texture of her curls before styling. Elena wore this unguarded state with the same grace she'd shown in her crimson dress.

"I'm glad," Elena said. She shifted slightly, adjusting

the sheet around her. "What does your morning usually look like?"

Claire considered the question. Her mornings were typically rushed affairs—throwing on clothes that wouldn't draw attention, minimal makeup applied with nervous hands, a quick breakfast if she remembered to eat at all.

"Nothing special," she said. "Coffee. Computer. Cat demanding attention."

Elena laughed, the sound warming the space between them. "Ah yes, Pixel with the one white paw. I can imagine her being quite insistent."

Claire felt a smile tugging at her lips. "She wakes me up by sitting on my chest and purring directly into my face. Very effective alarm clock."

Elena laughed, her voice full and inviting in the golden morning sun. "I'd really like to meet her one day." She stretched once more, lifting her arms above her head with effortless grace. "I'm starving after last night. Breakfast is definitely my favorite meal. There's a small café a few blocks away that serves the most amazing cinnamon brioche French toast you'll ever have."

The invitation hung in the air between them, unspoken but clear. Claire's stomach tightened. Breakfast. In public. Daylight. Her gaze flicked to the window where sunlight streamed through the gauzy curtains, harsh and revealing compared to the forgiving darkness of the club.

"I..." Claire hesitated, her fingers fidgeting with the edge of the silken sheet. The thought of walking into a crowded café, of being seen in the unforgiving morning light, of sitting across from someone as striking as Elena while other patrons stared and whispered—it sent a cold ripple of anxiety through her body. Last night had been different. The Glass Heel was a sanctuary, its shadows and amber light creating a space outside the ordinary world. But breakfast? That was real life. That was stepping back into a world that might not see her as she saw herself in this moment.

Elena studied her with those warm brown eyes, as if reading the hesitation in Claire's face. She smiled—not with pity, but with understanding.

"It's a lot to process," she said softly. "I remember my first morning after."

Claire nodded, grateful for the understanding. "It's not that I don't want to—"

"You don't need to explain," Elena said, touching Claire's hand briefly before sliding out from beneath the sheets.

Claire watched as Elena moved through the room with that same fluid grace she'd shown on the dance floor. The morning light loved her, gilding her bronze skin with gold as she gathered her clothes from where they'd fallen the night before. There was no awkwardness in her nakedness, no hurry to cover herself—just a woman completely at home in her body.

Elena slipped into her lace-trimmed underwear, the black fabric stark against her honey-gold skin, then pulled the crimson dress over her head. The silk—wrinkled now from its night on the floor—cascaded down her body like water finding its natural course, settling into the dips and curves of her waist and hips. She padded barefoot across the plush carpet to where her small beaded purse lay on the mahogany dresser and withdrew an ornate silver compact, its surface etched with swirling patterns. The compact opened with a soft click to reveal a lipstick the color of merlot in candlelight.

Claire expected her to apply it to her lips, parted slightly in concentration, but instead, Elena approached the full-length mirror that stood in the corner, its gilt frame catching the morning light.

With deliberate precision, she drew a string of numbers on the glass, the waxy lipstick making a soft scratching sound against the surface. Each digit stood out vividly against the clear pane, crimson as a fresh wound or a promise. "Ring me if you'd like breakfast," she said, her voice low and melodic in the quiet room. "Or if you simply want to hear your name spoken again." She twisted the lipstick down and returned it to the compact with a definitive snap.

Claire's heart fluttered beneath her ribs at the words, at the way Elena's mouth curved around them. The lipstick numbers caught the slanting morning light, gleaming slightly with a wet sheen as though still fresh from Elena's lips. The numbers stood there, bright and undeniable against the glass—seven digits that might lead anywhere or nowhere—an invitation without pressure. A choice.

"Take your time," Elena said, her voice soft as she leaned in to press a gentle kiss to Claire's cheek. "There's no rush."

Claire watched in silence as Elena meticulously gathered the rest of her belongings—her elegant small clutch, the delicate shoes she slipped onto her feet, and the shimmering pendant she gracefully draped back around her neck. The room felt transformed with Elena moving through it, as if her presence had altered the very essence of the air. The atmosphere seemed charged, vibrating gently with her every step, leaving a trail of subtle fragrance and a hint of warmth behind her.

"Thank you," Claire whispered, the words inadequate for what she truly meant.

Elena paused at the door, her hand on the ornate brass handle. "No," she said, her smile warm and knowing. "Thank you, Claire."

The door's soft click echoed in the hush, a punctuation mark on the night before, and then it was just

Claire, the honeyed spill of morning light, and the hush of a hotel room that still smelled faintly of perfume and sex and the citrusy tang of expensive soap. She sat motionless, the sheet drawn to her collarbones, knees propped like pale mountain ridges on the horizon of the mattress, beneath which her heart stuttered and ticked, unequal to the surge of her own feelings.

She listened for the sound of Elena's heels, their signature staccato tap, receding down the corridor. The echo faded by degrees, until all that remained was the rhythmic pulse of her own breath, the faint hum of pipes in the walls, and the distant city noise filtering through double-glazed windows. It didn't feel like absence so much as the anticipation of her own becoming, the way a canvas waits for the next brushstroke.

Claire waited until she was sure Elena was truly gone. Not just out of sight, but out of hearing range, out of the orbit of her gravity. Only then did she rise, the sheet falling away to expose the gooseflesh that bloomed across her arms and shoulders, a shiver of cold but also of sheer animal aliveness. Her bare feet pressed into the plush carpet, and she tiptoed to the window, hesitating at the threshold of sunlight, like a child peeking into a forbidden room.

With a flick of her wrist she drew the curtain aside, and the room was instantly flooded—no, saturated—with morning. The city outside was in full bloom: taxis nosing through intersections with feline patience, office workers scurrying in packs like urban starlings, the neon sign of a bakery across the street promising pastries and hot coffee. The flower vendor on the corner was already bustling, wrestling bouquets of daffodils and tulips into buckets, their colors so reckless and bright they looked like they'd been painted by a child. Claire watched him arrange and rearrange the stalks, fussing over details that no one else might notice, but which made the display perfect, just for its own sake.

She let the curtain fall and watched as the light became gentle again, filtered and forgiving, painting the room gold. In that light, everything seemed softer, truer. Even her own reflection, caught in the antique mirror above the desk, seemed more hers than ever. She caught sight of the smear of lipstick across the corner, precise as a signature, and the line of numbers—Elena's number—inscribed like an incantation.

She approached the dresser with slow, deliberate steps. Her dress—emerald green, still creased and rumpled from the night before—lay across the chair, draped as though on a sleeping lover. She ran her palm over the silk, feeling the memory of heat from her own body, and then just stood there for a long moment, regarding the woman in the glass. It was a strange sensation, to see herself so clearly and not flinch.

It wasn't the physical changes—that was the old illusion, that the body alone could be the battleground. There was the familiar scar near her hairline, the asymmetric arch of her brows, the smallness of her jaw offset by the fullness of her lips. But the difference was in the way she inhabited herself, in the way her posture had subtly shifted overnight: shoulders set farther back, chin slightly raised, like a guard let down after years of siege. She had not been rebuilt, just finally, mercifully unburdened of the need to disguise.

She lifted her hand, fingertips grazing the place where Elena's lips had left the faintest trace of desire on her collarbone, as though she could summon the sensation by memory alone. The skin there felt sensitized, like a page rubbed thin by repeated touch. She trailed her hand down, finding the echo of every place Elena had touched her: the hollow of her throat, the slope of her waist, the inside of her thigh. She shivered—a flush, a thrill—and hugged her arms around herself, uncertain whether she wanted to preserve the sensation or chase it away.

The drawer of the nightstand yielded her undies, neatly folded, and she stepped into them with a deliberateness that surprised her. She had always thought of her underthings as armor, a way of staking a claim on her own sense of self, even if the rest of the world couldn't see. Today, though, it felt less like armor and more like a celebration, a small, private act of defiance. She fastened her bra, cinching it into place with practiced hands, and felt her breathing steady. The emerald dress came next— she shook it out, inspected it for stains or runs, and then slipped it over her head. The silk hung differently this morning, or maybe it was Claire herself who'd shifted, but the effect was the same: the woman in the mirror was suddenly, shockingly, beautiful.

She had never thought of herself as beautiful. Passable, maybe, on a good day, if the light hit just so and she remembered to angle her chin. But the woman before her now was undeniably, heartbreakingly alive, the kind of beauty that came from motion, from the flush of blood beneath the surface. The chestnut hair (messy, yes, but vibrant), the eyes (a flash of green and gold), the jawline (softer than she'd wanted, once, now exactly right)—all of it came together, harmonized by the way she stood, by the way she dared to look herself in the eye.

There were, of course, the old doubts, like dust motes drifting in the beam of morning. Maybe this was just residual afterglow, the leftover charge of being seen so completely by someone else. Maybe she'd wake up tomorrow and the old anxiety would close in again, like a fist. But for now, at least, she let herself have this. She let herself have the morning, the dress, the warmth.

Her gaze drifted back to the lipstick numbers on the mirror. They were more than just a phone number—they were a challenge, a dare, a story waiting to be written. The digits themselves gleamed under the slanting sunlight, perfect and perverse, a secret language she was only just learning to read. Claire reached out, hovering her hand an inch from the glass, as though she could absorb the intent through osmosis.

Breakfast, Elena had said. Or just call to hear your name.

It was such a small, ordinary thing. But for Claire it felt monumental, like stepping through a door she'd spent years pressing her ear against, listening for any sound from the other side. What would she even say if she called? Last night had been dizzy with conversation, with touches and looks and the silent music of desire. But this—daylight, real life—demanded words, a currency in which Claire felt perpetually bankrupt.

She moved to the small desk, gathering her clutch and the few items she'd brought for the evening. The phone, battered at the edges and stuck with a sticker of a pixelated cat (Pixel herself, immortalized in holographic vinyl), was heavier than she remembered. She turned it over in her hand, considering the smoothness of its surface, the way it seemed to accumulate fingerprints and secrets.

Was Elena waiting for her to call? Was it a test, or a joke, or just a kindness offered to a woman who looked like she needed one? Claire's mind spun with possibilities, each one more fraught than the last. She could call and ruin everything, sound desperate or needy or—worse— delusional. Or she could not call, and spend the rest of her life wondering what might have happened if she'd had the nerve.

She popped the clasp on her clutch, searching for her compact (cheap, plastic, but reliable), and inspected her face in its tiny warped mirror. The remnants of last night's makeup still clung stubbornly to her lashes, a dark halo smudged beneath each eye. Instead of fixing it, she let it be. She wanted to remember how it felt, to wear the evidence of her night like a badge.

She tucked the compact away, then slipped her phone from the clutch and powered it on. The battery icon glowed red, warning her of its imminent death, but she ignored it. The phone booted, and for a moment she just stared at the lock screen—a picture of Pixel, mid-pounce, eyes wide as saucers—then thumbed in her code.

She glanced at the mirror, at the lipstick numbers. She memorized them in a glance, then typed them into her phone, careful not to transpose a single number.

Her thumb lingered over the Save button.

What would she say? Thank you for last night? I hope you got home safe? Would Elena even answer, or would it go to voicemail, that singular liminal space where intention and vulnerability collided?

For a moment, she let her thumb hover above the screen, eyes shut tight, savoring the indecision. She could almost hear the low rumble of Elena's voice in her ear, velvet-wrapped and humming with promise. Call me if you want to hear your name.

Claire held the phone in her hands as if it were some fragile, radiant artifact. Its surface was slick with the faintest sheen of nervous sweat, and she could see her own face reflected there: lips parted, eyes bright, the flush along her cheekbones a fever-map of desire and something perilously close to hope. She closed her eyes, willing the trembling of her fingers to still, and tried to summon herself back into her body. The phone felt heavier than before, as if the newly entered number had physical weight, as if each of Elena's digits pressed down on her with the density of a promise.

She unlocked the phone and the screen flared to life, illuminating the Rose Room in sharp relief. The walls—painted a deep, boozy burgundy—shivered with the sudden burst of blue light, and the copper tub in the corner gleamed in the dark like a penny that had just been minted. Claire sat on the edge of the bed, letting the mattress sag beneath her, and opened her contacts. She had to pause for a moment—her breath was coming too fast, shallow as a skipped stone—and she pressed her palm flat to her sternum as if she could slow her pulse by force.

What would she even say if Elena answered? The question unraveled in her mind with the speed and precision of a magician's trick. Would she say thank you for last night? Would she admit she couldn't stop thinking about her? Would she stumble, tongue-tied and clumsy, over any word that tried to capture the impossibility of what had happened in that room, between the sheets and the dawn? It felt like anything she said would be insufficient, a cheap translation of something that was already rare and perfect in its own original language.

But then she remembered the way Elena had spoken her name—Claire, with a curl of warmth around the r, a lift at the end that left the syllable floating in the air like a balloon. There had been no uncertainty in it, no hesitation, just a clear, crisp assertion: this is who you are, and I see you. The memory steadied her hand as she punched in the numbers, careful to check each digit twice against the lipstick signature on the mirror. When all ten were lined up in a little row of blue, she hesitated, finger poised above the "save." It felt ceremonial, almost sacred, as if she were inscribing something into the permanent record of the universe.

What was the right way to mark it? Just "Elena"? It seemed too casual for someone who had taken up so much space in her body, her mind, her future fantasies. "Elena from The Glass Heel" was too bureaucratic—a name you'd give to a hairdresser, or a landlord, or a distant cousin you saw only at funerals. So she typed, after a moment's deliberation, "Elena – Rose Room." It was a label and a memory, a secret code only the two of them could decipher. She pressed save before she could second-guess herself.

There. It was done. The number was real, a bridge between one night and whatever might come after. If she called, the connection would be instantaneous—she could imagine the pulse of her own voice vibrating at the other end, the possibility of Elena's laugh, the low thrum of recognition. But if she didn't call, the number would still exist, a seed in the soil of her phone, perhaps destined to sprout when the time was right. She liked that: the potential, the not-knowing.

She looked up, and the mirror across the room caught her gaze. She memorized the digits in a single glance, then turned away, needing to do something physical, something ordinary, to tether herself back to earth. Claire put the phone down and stood, feeling the blood return to her legs. She reached for her dress, still draped where she'd left it, and ran her hands over the silk, her fingers catching on the tiny, invisible snags left by the night.

For a long minute, she just stood there, dress in hand, body illuminated by morning sun and the faint golden wash from the sconce above the dresser. She traced the outline of her own shadow, elongated and distorted against the wall, and wondered if she would ever feel so entirely herself again. The memory of Elena's touch haunted her skin; she could still feel the imprint of hands on her waist, the careful brush of lips along the curve of her neck. The sensation was so visceral it made her shudder, and for a moment she almost sank back onto the bed, wanted to burrow herself deep beneath the sheets and let the world outside evaporate.

But she didn't. There was a kind of discipline in moving forward, in reaching for her clutch and gathering her things in a slow, deliberate inventory: wallet, compact mirror, lipstick (the same shade as the numbers on the glass), the slim silver case of breath mints that Elena had laughed at her for carrying. She lined them up along the edge of the desk, marveling at the banality of the objects in contrast to the wild, ungovernable emotions that still carouseled through her veins. She slipped the phone into the clutch last, feeling its outline press against her palm as she snapped the clasp shut.

Her eyes wandered once more to the mirror, and she tried to fix the room in her memory—the glint of gold filigree on the nightstand lamp, the swirl of rose petals someone (possibly housekeeping, possibly a hopeless romantic) had scattered over the coverlet, the half-empty bottle of water sweating onto the marble-topped dresser. Everything in the Rose Room felt curated, intentional, as if designed to capture and amplify whatever drama its guests enacted within its walls. Claire wondered how many other stories had played out here, how many numbers had been scrawled in lipstick and then wiped away with a careless hand.

She caught her own reflection and studied it for a beat, uncertain whether the woman staring back was a version she would recognize tomorrow, or the next day, or ever again. Her hair was wild—she'd given up trying to tame it after the third time Elena had buried her fingers in the tangles—but it framed her face in a way that was less "mess" than "statement." The dress fell in soft, gleaming folds over her hips, skimming the length of her thighs, and she could see the faint purple mark where Elena had pressed her mouth, just below the line of her collarbone. It felt like a trophy, a flag planted in new territory.

She reached for her compact, flicked it open, and regarded the smudges beneath her eyes. The mascara had migrated, leaving smears like war paint. Claire considered wiping it away, starting fresh, but then decided against it. She liked the look—the evidence of imperfection, the residue of what had happened. She applied a fresh layer of lipstick, tracing the line of her mouth with slow, careful precision, and then snapped the compact shut. She wanted to remember herself like this. Not flawless, but alive.

At the door, she hesitated, hand poised on the cool brass handle. There was a hush in the air, the kind of silence that comes only after something momentous has been said or done. She took one last, panoramic survey of the Rose Room—the tangle of sheets, the empty glasses on the nightstand, the shadow of Elena's scent on the air—and felt again that bittersweet ache, the knowledge that while the room had been the crucible for something extraordinary, it was also destined to be returned to its original, neutral state. She pressed her palm to the door, then turned the handle and stepped into the hallway.

The hallway stretched before her, empty and quiet, so different from last night when it had vibrated with promise. Claire's heels tapped a lonely rhythm on the hardwood as she made her way toward the spiral staircase. The photographs still watched her from their frames— women across decades who had found their own versions of freedom within these walls.

The staircase spiraled downward like a nautilus shell, each mahogany step taking her further from the perfumed sanctuary of the Rose Room. Her hand trailed along the wrought iron railing, cool and slightly pitted beneath her fingertips, worn smooth by thousands of hands before hers. The nightclub below came into view in cinematic fragments—first murky shadows, then angular shapes emerging from darkness, then the full expanse of The Glass Heel unfurling beneath her like a flower in reverse bloom.

It was transformed, stripped of its midnight glamour. Without the honey-amber lights and the bass that had vibrated through her ribcage, the space seemed both smaller and achingly vulnerable, like a theater set abandoned mid-performance. Bentwood chairs perched upside-down on marble-topped tables like sleeping birds, their legs pointing skyward. The polished cherrywood floor—scratched in places from countless stiletto heels—gleamed dully in the thin morning light filtering through dust-moted windows. The silence pressed against her eardrums with physical weight, a vacuum where last night's symphony of ice in glasses, breathless laughter, and the heartbeat rhythm of the DJ's careful selections had filled every molecule of air.

Claire paused at the bottom of the stairs, her gaze drawn magnetically to the far end of the horseshoe-shaped bar where she'd first seen Elena. The precise spot where the crimson-dressed woman had materialized behind her like an apparition from another era, voice like honey poured over river stones. Now the bar stood empty, a crescent moon of polished ebony. Crystal glasses gleamed in neat, military rows on glass shelves, bottles of amber and clear liquids catching what little light penetrated the space, transforming ordinary alcohol into liquid jewels.

Her feet carried her across the dance floor without conscious direction, heels clicking a solitary percussion against the wood. The massive disco ball hung motionless overhead like a suspended planet, its thousand mirrored facets dulled to the color of tarnished silver without the spotlights to ignite them. Last night, it had spun with dizzying abandon, casting kaleidoscopic fragments of light across Elena's flushed cheekbones and parted lips as they moved together in the crush of bodies. Claire closed her eyes briefly, feeling again the phantom pressure of Elena's hand at the small of her back, five distinct points of heat guiding her through turns she hadn't known her body could make, her spine arching like a violin string beneath expert fingers.

She opened her eyes and turned toward the row of sapphire-blue velvet booths along the western wall. The third one—she remembered with cartographer's precision—where Elena had leaned in close enough that Claire could count individual eyelashes, and asked in a voice barely audible above the music if she could kiss her. Where Claire had nodded, not trusting her voice to emerge as anything but a desperate croak. Where their lips had met for the first time, soft and tentative then hungry, and something inside her chest had finally, mercifully clicked into place like the tumbler of a lock.

The booth looked ordinary now. Just velvet upholstery the color of midnight oceans and a small table bearing rings from forgotten drinks, nothing to suggest it had been the site of such seismic transformation. Claire's fingers brushed the back of the booth as she passed, the velvet cool and slightly rough against her skin, catching on a hangnail she hadn't noticed before.

She made her way to the exit, each step measured and deliberate as a tightrope walker. The heavy oak door that had seemed so intimidating last night—a portal to another world—now yielded easily to her push, hinges singing a soft metallic note. Sunlight flooded in like spilled champagne, momentarily blinding after the dim interior. She blinked rapidly, eyes watering, adjusting to the brightness of a day that seemed impossibly ordinary after the magic of the night before.

Chapter 6

Ascent

The morning greeted her with a sharp, swirling gust—so much colder and more immediate than she remembered. For a heartbeat she simply stood, letting the shock of the air make her shiver, the skin of her face prickling, eyes stinging with the sudden clarity of it. The city's sounds pressed closer now, their pitch higher, the world outside more urgent than the one she'd left behind. She clutched the collar of her faux wool coat tighter around her throat, half-expecting the velvet roar of The Glass Heel to follow her into the street. But it didn't: the door swung shut on its own slow hinge, closing with a muffled bass thud that left the sidewalk as silent as a new sheet of paper.

For one odd moment, Claire hesitated in the vestibule between then and now. Beyond the stoop, the city pulsed with a different perfume—diesel, salt brine, the faint iron tang of snow waiting to fall. She breathed deep, letting the two worlds intermingle in her lungs. Behind her, the lock turned with a heavy, deliberate click. The finality of it sent a tremor up her spine, as if the sound had drawn a line between every version of herself that existed before and after this night.

The sidewalk was unspoiled, blank as a fresh canvas. Snow had fallen reckless and heavy during her hours inside, transforming the cracked concrete into a luminous white runway. Streetlights made the drifts glitter like sugar frosting; the footprints of earlier passersby were already vanished, lost to the city's soft erasure. Claire hovered for a second above this untouched expanse, boots poised at the edge, unready to be the first to disturb it. She looked back at the door—just once, quickly—as if expecting someone to burst out and call her by name. No one did. The opaque glass reflected only the curved brass of the handle, and faintly, her own pale outline. The world in there had closed its doors for the night. The world out here was waiting for her.

She stepped forward, and the snow gave way with a precise, satisfying crunch. The sound felt clean, ceremonial, almost like applause. With each step, Claire's legs remembered the impossible rhythm of last night's tangled sheets—the way Elena's fingers had traced the hollow of her hip bone, how they'd moved together in the half-light, their shadows merging on the wall. She glanced up at the fogged windows above the street, wondering if Elena was still there, watching her leave. A part of her— small, but stubborn—hoped that was true.

By the corner, her cheeks already burned with cold, and her breath made little silver ghosts that vanished as soon as she exhaled. She pressed her knuckles to her lips, finding them still sore from Elena's kisses. The memory rewrote itself on her mouth, fresh as the chill, and Claire smiled to herself. She tried to remember the feeling of those moments—Elena's lipstick, the delicate scrape of teeth, the warm tongue teasing the seam of her mouth. It was almost easy to recall now, easier than she would have thought. Maybe it would stay with her this time, as a keepsake. Maybe nothing would be able to take it back.

She skirted a patch of ice, boots unsteady, an echo of the first time she'd walked in heels. How many nights ago had that been? Three, maybe four. It felt like ages, each day a small exile from the girl she had become inside the club's velvet walls. But today—today she felt the difference, felt the shift under her skin, the way her body belonged to itself at last. Her shadow, too, moved with new confidence—longer, leaner, unafraid of the streetlights.

Around her, the city was waking up. A baker flipped his sign from CLOSED to OPEN, steam billowing from the vents behind his shop. The eastern sky had lightened to the color of weak tea, silhouetting the L tracks where a lone train rattled past. A siren wailed somewhere, then faded. Claire listened to it disappear, replaced by the faint, tinny music of her own pulse. The fear that usually stalked her at this early hour—of being seen, of being known, of being followed—was absent. Instead she held herself upright, shoulders back, chin lifted. The rhythm of her step matched the cadence of delivery trucks rumbling to life, of shopkeepers sweeping their stoops: for the first time, she moved through the awakening city as though she belonged to its morning.

At the next block, she turned and glanced back. The Glass Heel's sign hung dark, its neon letters extinguished, but the building stood out—the only structure on the block with so much as a hint of glamour. Above the entryway, the stained glass in the old theater window glowed faintly, a leftover warmth from the revelry inside. Claire felt a squeeze in her chest, half pain and half gratitude. It was so easy to romanticize sanctuary spaces, to think of them as holy. But the club had been a kind of church for her, the altar where she'd knelt to be forgiven for the sin of wanting.

A trio of strangers hurried past her, heads down, scarves pulled tight. One of them looked up, eyes quick and bright, and offered a nod. Claire returned it—small, reflexive, but real. She felt a thrill of connection, a flash of belonging that made her want to laugh for no reason. She made a mental note to remember this: that it was possible to stand in the open, in the cold, in her own skin, and not be afraid.

She pressed onward. Each block she crossed felt like a chapter in some new, uncharted story. A delivery truck rumbled past, its headlights cutting yellow paths through the lingering dark. Behind a steamed deli window, a figure moved, stacking fresh bagels. She imagined the city as a vast witness stirring from sleep, all its windows and alleys watching her without judgment as they blinked awake.

She moved from streetlight to streetlight, pausing beneath one where a barista unlocked the front door of a café, the smell of brewing coffee escaping into the cold. Snowflakes settled on her face, delicate, nothing like the weighted flakes in her childhood memory. They melted instantly on her warm cheeks as the eastern sky lightened from black to navy. She let them fall, unbothered, liking the way they vanished on contact, leaving only a brief tingle behind.

For a long while, she simply walked, letting her mind drift. She thought of Elena, of the scent of whiskey on her breath and the velvet press of her palms. She thought of the laughter she'd shared with Julian behind the bar, his soft jokes and the way he always found the perfect song to fill an awkward silence. She thought of Echo—regal, unshakeable Echo—who had welcomed her to the club on that first trembling night, and who had watched, always watched, as if she could see the shape of what Claire might become.

And, inevitably, Claire thought of herself. The girl who had arrived at The Glass Heel so desperate for transformation, who had been terrified she would never measure up—and who had found, in the end, that there was nothing to measure. That there was only the truth of being here, alive, and wanting.

She reached the end of the block, and the city seemed to rise up to meet her. The snow continued to fall, softening the edges of everything, but Claire's steps only grew surer. She didn't need to look back at the club, or at the person she used to be. She carried both forward now, tucked inside her like a secret.

Above her, in a window, a silhouette shifted. Claire didn't know who watched her from the other side of that glass, but she imagined it was someone who understood.

Echo Dela Cruz's bare feet touched the cold hardwood as she slid from tangled sheets, the indent of her head still warm on the pillow. She pulled a silk robe around her shoulders and padded across her fourth-floor suite above The Glass Heel, leaving the lamp unlit. The first gray suggestion of dawn filtered through frost-laced windows. She pressed two sleep-creased fingers to the glass, her exhale creating a thin breath of fog that haloed her reflection.

Below, Claire's silhouette cut across the fresh snow. Echo squinted, still blinking sleep from her eyes, watching the girl's gait shift from tentative to bold with each step away from the club. Claire's insufficient coat wrapped tight around her like armor, collar up against the wind. Even from this height, Echo could make out the set of those shoulders—no longer cowering. Echo's lips flickered in a smile as she reached for the half-empty wine glass she'd abandoned hours before.

She sipped, grimacing at the room-temperature cabernet, and studied the street more carefully. The city was beginning to stir—a delivery truck rumbling past, a distant train clacking against cold rails, someone sweeping their stoop. Echo's toes curled against the floor as she shifted her weight. The Glass Heel below stood dark and quiet, but she knew the real work happened in these liminal hours, when girls like Claire carried its magic out into the waking world—magic still brittle, still trembling, still prone to shattering if not handled with care.

Across the street, something shifted in the shadow near the flower shop. A figure—tall, hunched, wrapped in an oversized parka—paced a tight circle in the slush. Echo's eye for detail (so finely honed it bordered on supernatural) caught the nervous rhythm of the person's hands, the way anxieties telegraphed themselves through posture before they ever reached the surface of speech. The shape registered instantly: a girl, perhaps a young woman, standing at the blurry edge of her own story. Her head was bowed, hair tucked messily under a beanie, and she hunched over a phone that wasn't quite enough to anchor or distract her. She kept sneaking glances at The Glass Heel's sign, as if hoping it might reignite and offer her a reason to step inside.

Echo knew that look. She had seen it for decades—on rainy nights, in deep winter, at the dawn of June when the city's queer population blossomed with urgent color. The look was always the same: I want to belong, but I don't know how. Sometimes the girls crossed the street and approached the door. Sometimes they hovered until dawn, then slinked away, convinced they'd been rejected by fate itself. Echo watched this girl and found herself wishing, not for the first time, that there was a gentler on-ramp to the kind of belonging The Glass Heel offered. She supposed that was why her own heart never quite softened, no matter how many transformations she witnessed. Every new story was as dangerous and as precious as the last.

A small fixation: the pendant at Echo's throat, a single glass heel, caught the morning light and scattered it across her sternum. She fingered it in silence, letting the chill of the window and the heat of her wine balance each other in her bloodstream. In the reflection, she caught sight of herself—not as the world saw her, but as she truly appeared: regal, commanding, sharp at the edges, but always measured. The years had not dulled her, only clarified the contours of who she was meant to be.

She turned her gaze back to the street, watching as Claire's figure receded, shrinking with distance but amplifying in significance. From four stories up, the girl's footprints marked a delicate calligraphy across the snow, a visible proof of passage. Echo saw herself in that trajectory—a girl who had once walked out into a world that was not meant for her, and had returned, time and again, until it bent. She wondered if Claire sensed this lineage, the invisible thread that connected each new fledgling to the matriarchs and queens who had come before. Probably not, she thought, but it didn't matter. The inheritance was there nonetheless.

Echo's reverie broke as the hunched girl across the street began to move, pulled by some faint hope or perhaps just a momentary surge of desperation. She shuffled forward, boots slipping on the curb, then stopped just short of the club's stoop. The sign above was dim now—no beacon to welcome or warn—but the girl still raised her head and stared at the door, as if waiting for it to speak to her directly. For a long, still moment, the girl stood there, motionless, her breath visible against the glass. Then, as if startled by this hopefulness, she retreated two steps, fumbled for her phone, and began typing furiously, perhaps to a friend, a stranger, maybe even to herself.

Echo watched the entire drama unfold as if it were a silent play performed just for her. The urge to intervene was always present—sometimes she did, descending the stairs with the queenly grace her patrons expected, offering a cigarette or a word or just the warmth of presence. But tonight she trusted the city to do its work. The snow was a cleansing force, the night a crucible. The girl would come when she was ready, or she would not. The world spun either way.

Echo swirled her wine and raised the glass in a private salute to the girl on the street, to Claire, to all the iterations of herself that lingered in the city's memory. She tipped the glass to her lips and whispered, "Another girl who came to be seen… and left with something more." The words hung in the room, half mantra, half benediction.

The morning was fresh and the air was thinner than it had any right to be, scoured of all but the faintest traces of diesel, fried oil, and the yawned-out ozone of a city winding down. Claire walked steadily through the drifting, fine-grained snow, each step etching a crisp negative into the blank sidewalk that the wind and the next hour would erase. She moved with the kind of careful self-possession that came after the performance had ended, when the last spotlight cut off and the world shrank back to inconvenient size. She counted her breaths—slow, deliberate, even as her pulse jittered with the residue of too many firsts. She was fifteen minutes from the Blue Line station, fifteen minutes from the uncurtained anonymity of public transit, and she measured every block like a rationed sweetness: fifteen, then fourteen, then thirteen, and so on, each step both a shedding of the night and a secret preservation of it in her marrow.

Behind her, the dome of The Glass Heel receded quickly, its name nothing but a haunted glimmer in the snow-stippled dark. She did not look back. The club had been both sanctuary and crucible—she could feel it in the set of her jaw, in the gentle ache at her thighs, in the smudge of lipstick she worried at with the tip of her tongue. If she turned, she feared the magic would collapse into something brittle and desperate, so she pressed onward, clutching her coat close with one hand and a borrowed confidence with the other.

The city breathed differently on a Saturday morning—steam curling from rusty manhole covers into pale winter light, the hiss of an occasional bus braking at a near-empty corner. Sidewalks were quiet, broken only by the shuffle of bundled figures heading to early shifts or corner cafés. Delivery trucks growled past patches of snow, their taillights blinking in the stillness like tired eyes. Chicago at seven on a weekend was slow to wake, its heartbeat steady, its windows still heavy-lidded. Claire matched her breath to its unhurried rhythm, surprised at how naturally she could belong to this gentler pulse. The cold sharpened her senses, carrying the mingled scents of diesel, coffee, and fresh bread drifting from a nearby panadería. She was tired, but she was not hollow.

Her body felt different. Her body felt—here, at last, she could admit it—like hers. There had been no physical transformation, not really; the hormones were still too new to have rendered any visible changes, and her padding and tuck would soon enough be undone by the heat of her own apartment. But in that moment, the little ripples of sensation—the sway of her hips, the brush of synthetic hair grazing her bare neck, the soft hiss of tights beneath her skirt—became not an alien theater but an intimate, private language. She understood, suddenly, the difference between wearing a mask and inhabiting a role: the former suffocates, the latter liberates. She knew she would have to put the mask back on tomorrow, but for now, the role was her own.

She passed the slumped awning of a shuttered diner, the kind with neon in the window and an all-night promise it could not keep. Its reflection doubled her in the glass: two Claires, one shadowed in sodium yellow, one in the cold fluorescence of the streetlamp. She paused there, drinking in the sight—her own figure backlit by the city, half aspirational and half realized. The lipstick was smeared at one corner, a telltale streak that would once have sent her spiraling into self-consciousness. Now, it was evidence. She was here. She had done something. The memory of Elena's thumb smoothing her lip, the press of a hot palm at the hinge of her jaw, flickered and held. "There you are," Elena had murmured, not as a question, but as a simple statement of fact. Claire had tried to protest—to offer a nervous laugh, to deflect—but she'd been caught in the gravity of Elena's certainty, and for a moment it had been enough.

The snow thickened as she made her way east, past a row of pawn shops and payday lenders whose metal security grates were painted with crude murals: a wolf howling at the moon, a ballerina poised en pointe, a row of dominoes collapsing one after another. Claire read them like a secret chronicle of the city's underlife—aspiration, grace, inevitability. She wondered what her own mural would be, if she could choose. A girl walking alone at night, unafraid? A glass slipper shattering on concrete, its shards scattering into stars? She smiled at the thought, knowing how melodramatic it sounded even as she cherished it.

She stopped at a crosswalk, the traffic light's red hand blinking in warning. Two men stood across the street, one slouched against a mailbox, the other gesturing animatedly with a cigarette. Their voices drifted over, half-garbled, but Claire caught the word "princess" and braced herself for the sharp edge of ridicule. Instead, the men barely glanced her way as she passed, already sinking into their argument over sports, or money, or the next place to land. Claire's body unclenched in stages. She realized how much tension she still carried, how much of her effort went into anticipating threats that, tonight at least, failed to materialize.

There were moments—at the beginning of her transition, in the dim-lit purgatory of the men's restroom at work or in the gauntlet of her parents' questions—when Claire had doubted if this could ever be more than an audition. She'd rehearsed her gestures, her voice, the tilt of her head, all in service of convincing some imagined jury that she deserved to exist. But the city at this hour gave her the gift of forgetfulness. No one asked her to justify herself. The world was too busy thawing its own hungers, too indifferent to play judge. For the first time in a long while, Claire felt less like an imposter and more like someone with a legitimate claim to the sidewalk under her feet.

She moved, block by block, through the territory of her own becoming.

At a corner, she stopped to dig a ChapStick from her purse. Her hands shook a little from the cold, but she managed the cap with only minor fumbling. As she applied it—careful, precise, determined to undo the evidence of her prior undoing—it occurred to her that this, too, was a ritual of autonomy. She did not need to look presentable for anyone but herself. She laughed, a brief, crystalline sound that startled a pigeon from its perch atop a streetlight. The bird fluttered, then settled, unbothered by her presence.

She felt herself changing with every step, like a Polaroid, image resolving from gray to sharp. She took stock of her physical sensations: the slight ache in her calves from the unfamiliar height of her heels, the way her feet numbed and then burned with each alternation of cold and friction. She had learned quickly how to walk without looking like she was learning; the trick was to pretend you'd always been this way, to never look down, to let the city rearrange itself around you. She was getting better at it.

A memory flashed: Echo at the bar, her eyes dark and appraising, saying, "You'll find the world is more resilient than you expect. Including you." At the time, Claire had been too distracted by the pulse of the club and the nearness of Elena to really listen. Now, she replayed the words and found they fit her like a glove. She repeated them under her breath, a mantra, letting the syllables warm her teeth. She was resilient. She was expected. The city would bend, if she pushed just hard enough.

By the time she reached the station's perimeter, a hush had settled over the city, the kind of silence that accrued only in the stillness of morning, after even the cabs had not started to prowl for fares. Snowflakes slanted through the orange glow of the sodium lamps, swirling in the updrafts from the subway grates. Claire moved with a singular focus, her body thrumming with the residue of the night, a charge that made every sensation sharper and stranger than it had any right to be.

She almost missed the shape on the stoop—a figure folded in on herself, half-hidden behind the balustrade of a crumbling brownstone. In the thin winter light, she was nearly erased by the snow, but certain details caught Claire's eye: the wiry tension of arms locked around blue-jeaned knees; the shimmer of cheap eyeshadow worn like armor; the chipped, deliberate lipstick applied with the kind of care reserved for survival's most sacred rituals. The girl couldn't have been more than nineteen. Her story was there in the scatter of faint bruises on her arms and in the way she tracked Claire's approach with the cautious intelligence of a stray animal.

It was too late for the sanctuary of The Glass Heel. Saturday at this hour was a liminal place—caught between the night's last shadows and the day's first demands. Claire knew this in-between all too well: the waiting, the quiet ache for proof that another body could move freely through the world so yours might have permission to do the same. She recognized the posture most of all—shoulders caved, chin tucked, every inch of the body negotiated into something provisional, something that might pass unnoticed. To the casual eye, the girl was invisible; to someone fluent in the code, she was a flare in the snow.

Claire slowed but didn't stop. The unwritten rules were clear—no intrusion, no questions, no sudden offers that might feel like traps. As she passed, their eyes met for a single heartbeat. Claire gave her a small, uneven smile. Not comfort, not pity—just recognition. I see you. You exist.

The girl did not return the smile. But her gaze stayed locked on Claire's, unblinking, hungry, refusing to cede the point. As Claire mounted the first step to the Blue Line entrance, she felt the stare following her like a thread, tethering her back to the stoop, to the city, to the collective memory of everyone who'd ever waited in the cold for their turn at safety.

Inside the vestibule, the sudden heat was as shocking as a slap. Claire took a moment to shed her gloves and undo the top button of her coat, letting the air hit her skin. Her reflection ghosted in the plexiglass, overlaying her face with a faint tracery of graffiti and old, sun-faded stickers. She studied herself: the unevenness of foundation on her jawline, the mascara smudge that had crept into the hollow beneath her left eye, the faint puckering of her upper lip where she'd bitten it raw in the bathroom hours before. For years, these artifacts of imperfection would have sent her spiraling—now, she catalogued them with a forensic interest, as if examining evidence of someone she used to be.

The stairs to the elevated platform were slick with a thin layer of meltwater, every step a negotiation between traction and disaster. Claire climbed with a practiced grace, one hand curled around the metal handrail, heels clicking a steady rhythm that echoed through the empty stairwell. At the top, the wind hit her again, slicing clean through her coat and driving an involuntary shiver down the length of her spine. But she didn't hunch against it, didn't draw in on herself as she once would have. She straightened, squared her shoulders, and stepped out into the open.

The platform lights were merciless—no forgiving candleglow, no velvet shadows to lend mystery or allure. Just the bare white glare that made every feature ruthlessly explicit, every flaw in makeup and posture illuminated for the city to see. Claire realized, with something like amusement, that she'd spent most of her life dreading this exact moment: to be seen unvarnished, to have nothing but herself as buffer between the world and her trembling, newly minted identity.

This morning, though, she found she didn't mind. She let her gaze drift over the platform, taking in the other late-night travelers: a dozing man in construction boots, a pair of teenage boys play-fighting over headphones, a middle-aged woman in a parka hunched over a Styrofoam cup, muttering into her phone. No one spared Claire more than a glance. No one cared what she was, or how she looked, or whether she was real enough to deserve the space she occupied. She was just another body in transit, another note in the city's midnight chord.

The train was running late, as always. Claire wrapped her arms around herself and rocked gently on her heels, feeling the vibration of the city's machinery through the boards beneath her feet. She thought of the girl on the stoop, and then—unbidden—of every other girl who'd stood on platforms like this, in every city, in every year, waiting to be carried forward by the indifferent tides of steel and electricity.

The memory of The Glass Heel lingered: bodies pressed together on the dance floor, her hips caught in the current of Elena's rhythm, both of them slick with sweat under the pulsing lights. Later, in the Rose Room, where the wallpaper bloomed with faded crimson patterns and the sheets smelled faintly of lavender and someone else's perfume. She remembered how Elena's fingertips had traced her collarbone in the half-light.

The wind built in increments, tugging at her hair and making her eyes water. She let it, blinking into the sting. For so long, she'd been afraid of being seen—by men on the street, by old classmates, by her parents, by herself. But as the minutes ticked by and the cold bit deeper, she felt something inside her shift. The fear was still there, but it was joined now by a kind of stubborn pride, a refusal to disappear no matter how much the world might prefer it.

The construction worker snored and woke himself with a snort, then glared blearily at Claire as if she'd invented the noise for her own amusement. She smiled at him, tentative and genuine, and was surprised when he shrugged, offered a halfhearted smile in return, and went back to his nap. This, too, was a kind of arrival: the casual acceptance of strangers, the luxury of being ignored.

The train announced itself with a high, Doppler-whined shriek, headlamps throwing monstrous shadows down the length of the track. The Blue Line was always the same—ancient, battered, smelling of ozone and wet wool, the interiors graffiti-scarred and sticky with the residue of a thousand commuter meals. Claire stepped into the car without pausing at the threshold, the action so automatic she barely noticed the lack of hesitation that had once accompanied every public entrance.

Inside, the benches were cold and mostly unoccupied. She slid into a corner seat, arranged her coat around her knees, and exhaled. The doors closed with a pneumatic shudder, and the train lurched forward, resuming its journey through the awaking city.

Chapter 7

Tracks and Tremors

Four other passengers occupied the car. A nurse in wrinkled scrubs dozed against the window, her ID badge still clipped to her pocket. A middle-aged man with salt-and-pepper stubble held The Sun-Times like a shield, his eyes flicking above the newsprint as Claire settled into her seat. Across the aisle, a young couple leaned into each other, fingers intertwined, whispering with the conspiratorial intimacy of those who've been up all night.

Claire felt the man's gaze linger on her throat, her hands, her knees. She knew what he was looking for—the telltale signs, the incongruities he could catalog and file away. Six months ago, his scrutiny would have sent her spiraling, made her shrink into herself like a turtle retreating into its shell. She would have crossed her legs differently, pitched her voice higher, overcompensated in a dozen small ways.

Not today.

She met his eyes steadily, her posture relaxed yet dignified. After a moment, he returned to his newspaper with a small, dismissive shrug. Claire didn't care. The victory wasn't in changing his mind—it was in realizing his opinion had never mattered in the first place.

The train lurched forward, its ancient frame groaning as it pulled away from the station. Claire watched the city blur past, the early dawn streets empty except for delivery trucks and taxis. The rhythm of the tracks created a hypnotic backdrop to her thoughts, which kept circling back to the night at The Glass Heel, to Elena's hands on her waist, to the way she'd felt completely seen for the first time.

The nurse across from her startled awake as the train hit a rough patch of track. She blinked, disoriented, then caught Claire's eye and offered a weary smile before checking her watch and sighing. Claire wondered what her story was—how many hours she'd been on her feet, how many lives she'd touched, what small kindnesses she'd offered to strangers in sterile rooms.

Six months ago, Claire would have been too self-conscious to notice anyone else's exhaustion. She would have been too busy wondering if the nurse could tell, if she was staring, if she was silently judging. Now she found herself wondering instead if the nurse had eaten, if she had someone waiting at home, if her feet ached as badly as Claire's did in these kitten heels.

The train slowed as it approached the next station. The couple stood, still holding hands, and moved toward the doors. The girl—barely twenty, with pink hair and combat boots—glanced back at Claire, her eyes lingering for a moment on Claire's berry-stained lips. There was no judgment in her gaze, just a flash of recognition, like one traveler in a strange city recognizing another who spoke her language.

Claire looked back at the young woman, acknowledging the moment with a slight nod before the doors closed between them. The train lurched forward again, carrying her deeper into the early morning.

As she settled back in her seat, Claire found herself studying the remaining passengers with new curiosity. The nurse had pulled a protein bar from her bag, unwrapping it with the mechanical movements of someone too tired to even register hunger. Dark circles shadowed her eyes, and her scrubs bore faint stains—coffee, perhaps, or something less innocuous from her shift. How many patients had she tended to tonight? How many hands had she held, how many wounds had she dressed?

The man with the newspaper turned a page with a sharp crackle. His wedding ring caught the fluorescent light as he adjusted his grip. The paper was folded precisely at the business section, his eyes scanning figures and percentages with practiced efficiency. His shoes were polished but worn at the heels, suggesting a life of routine and steady persistence.

Claire realized with a start that she wasn't watching them to gauge their reactions to her. She wasn't monitoring for signs of discomfort or judgment. For the first time, she was simply seeing them as people with their own stories, their own exhaustions and triumphs, completely separate from her existence.

The nurse's phone buzzed. She glanced at it, and her tired face softened with a smile as she typed a quick response. To a partner, perhaps? A child? Someone was waiting for her, someone who knew the weight of the hours she carried.

The realization settled in Claire's chest like a warm stone: The Glass Heel had changed her in ways beyond the physical pleasure of Elena's touch or the thrill of being desired. It had shifted something fundamental in how she positioned herself in the world. She was no longer merely an object to be scrutinized, but a subject doing the scrutinizing—a full participant in the human exchange of seeing and being seen.

For the next forty-five minutes, Claire occupied herself with a kind of anthropological interest, watching as her fellow riders came and went with the silent choreography of the early city. At each stop, the doors shuddered open to admit new faces: an elderly woman wearing a Cubs scarf and orthopedic sneakers, three construction workers with lunchboxes and hard hats, a quartet of giggling teenagers with backpacks slung low and hair mussed from sleep. Some stayed for a handful of stops; others, for only a single lurch and a blur of city blocks.

She took in the small details that hinted at entire lives: the careful way the old woman nestled her purse close, as if it were a pet; the heavy banter of the workers, which masked an underlying fatigue; the way one of the teenagers, a boy with delicate features and badly bitten nails, kept sneaking glances at his phone and then at another boy across the aisle. Claire wondered if this was his first crush, whether the anticipation felt bright and sick in his stomach the way it used to in hers.

Sometimes, the train car would empty around her for a few stops, leaving only the rhythmic hum of the rails and the neon flicker of passing streetlights. Other times, the crowd thickened suddenly—a pulse of humanity pressed together, exuding the scent of cologne, shampoo, and sleep. Claire observed, but didn't withdraw. She let herself belong to the anonymous tide, invisible and unremarkable, if only for the length of a commute.

With each stop, her own sense of self seemed to become less about the sharp edges she so often policed and more about a gentle curiosity toward the world outside her. She found herself easing her posture, her hands falling into her lap, her breath deepening in time with the train's rocking. Nobody was staring. Nobody cared. Or rather, they cared about their own burdens, their own secret narratives, and that was comfort enough.

Near Western, the teenagers tumbled out in a tangle, trailed by one of the workers who separated from the others with a wave. At California, the old woman heaved herself upright and shuffled toward the door, pausing only to nod at Claire as she passed. Claire nodded back, a small, silent communion.

By the time her own stop approached, the car had emptied again except for the nurse, who had dozed off with her head bobbing, and the man with the newspaper, who appeared to be rereading the same page obsessively. The city outside had brightened to a frost-tinted dawn, the snow at the curbsides now tinged with the pink of awakening, the blue line tracing its elevated arc toward Logan Square.

The train slowed for Logan Square station. Claire gathered her purse and stood, steadying herself against the pole as the brakes squealed. The nurse had fallen back asleep, her protein bar half-eaten in her lap. The newspaper man didn't look up as Claire passed.

Outside, the air was bracingly cold, the sky just beginning to lighten at its edges. The familiar scent of her neighborhood greeted her—coffee from the 24-hour diner, the sweet cinnamon warmth from the Mexican bakery where workers were already preparing the day's first batch of pan dulce, the faint metallic tang of snow threatening to fall.

Each step on the icy pavement rang out like a declaration as Claire made her way home. The sound of her heels—once a source of anxiety—now felt like ownership. This sidewalk. This neighborhood. This life. Hers.

Dawn painted her building's brick facade with amber light as Claire approached the entrance. Her fingers found the familiar keypad, muscle memory guiding them through the security code. The door clicked open, revealing the stairwell that would carry her, step by weary step, up three flights to her apartment—the building's developers having deemed an elevator an unnecessary luxury.

By the time she reached her door on the third floor, her calves burned with the sweet exhaustion of the night's revelry. Keys jingled in her hand as the familiar scratching began on the other side. She barely had the door open before Pixel shot through the gap, a streak of fur and need, figure-eighting between her ankles with that distinctive white paw flashing like a tiny beacon.

"I know, I know. I'm late," Claire said, bending down to scratch behind the cat's ears. "Did you miss me?"

Pixel's purr rumbled against her palm, a small engine of forgiveness. The apartment was just as she'd left it— dishes in the sink, laptop open on the coffee table, yesterday's clothes draped over the back of a chair. But it felt different somehow, as if the space had contracted in her absence, grown smaller against the expanding universe she'd discovered at The Glass Heel.

Claire slipped out of her coat and kicked off her heels with a sigh of relief. Her feet throbbed as blood rushed back into compressed toes. She padded to the bedroom, Pixel trailing close behind, vocalizing her complaints about the long night alone.

In her bedroom, Claire unzipped the emerald dress, letting it slide to the floor in a whisper of silk. She stood for a moment in her underwear, examining herself in the full-length mirror mounted on her closet door. The marks Elena had left were fading now—small crescents where fingernails had pressed into skin, a faint purple bloom at the junction of neck and shoulder. Claire touched each one gently, cataloging them like artifacts from a sacred excavation.

She pulled on her softest sweatpants and an oversized t-shirt from a concert she'd never actually attended. The cotton felt strange against her skin after a night wrapped in silk, but the comfort was welcome. She scrubbed the makeup from her face with gentle circular motions, watching as her "going out" self dissolved into the more familiar contours of her everyday face.

Back in the living room, she collapsed onto the couch. Pixel immediately jumped into her lap, kneading her thighs with rhythmic intensity before settling into a tight ball of contentment. Outside, the city was fully awake now, sunlight streaming through her blinds in sharp golden blades.

Claire closed her eyes, but instead of darkness, she saw Elena—the curve of her smile, the intensity of her gaze as she'd guided Claire's hands to places Claire had never dared touch before. She felt again the press of Elena's lips against her throat, heard the whispered affirmations that had made her body arch with pleasure and recognition.

"She saw me, Pixel," Claire murmured to the cat, who blinked slowly in response. "Really saw me."

The memory of Elena's number, written in lipstick on the mirror, flashed through her mind. She'd carefully entered it into her phone before leaving the Rose Room, but hadn't yet found the courage to call. The phone felt heavy in her hand as she picked it up from the coffee table, swiping to unlock the screen. Her thumb hovered over Elena's name in her contacts.

What if last night had been a dream? What if Elena answered and didn't remember her? What if she did remember but regretted everything in the harsh light of day?

Pixel headbutted her hand, purring loudly, as if urging her forward.

"You're right," Claire whispered. "What's the worst that could happen?"

Her heart pounded as she pressed the call button, each ring stretching into eternity. Then—

"Hello?" Elena's voice was warm honey through the speaker, slightly rough around the edges as if she'd just woken up.

"Elena. It's Claire," she said, surprised by the steadiness in her own voice. "From last night."

A soft chuckle. "I remember exactly who you are, Claire."

The sound of her name in Elena's mouth sent a shiver down Claire's spine, just as it had in the Rose Room. She closed her eyes, letting the sensation wash over her.

"I was thinking about your breakfast invitation," Claire said, curling her bare toes into the carpet. "And I realized I'm more of a dinner person than a breakfast person. Would you like to have dinner with me tonight?"

There was a moment of silence – just long enough for Claire's heart to stutter – before Elena answered.

"I'd like that very much," she said, and Claire could hear the smile in her voice.

Relief flooded through her, warm and sweet as sunlight. "Eight o'clock? There's a little Italian place near me that makes incredible risotto."

"Perfect. Text me the address," Elena said. "And Claire?"

"Yes?"

"I'm glad you called."

After they hung up, Claire remained motionless on

the plush couch, the phone clutched tightly to her chest as a warm, radiant smile slowly spread across her face. Her eyes sparkled with joy, and her heart fluttered with excitement. Meanwhile, Pixel, her fluffy tabby cat, meowed with an air of indignation, his soft fur bristling as he demanded the attention that had been diverted from him for far too long. Claire chuckled softly, the sound like a gentle melody, and reached over to scratch behind Pixel's ears. His purrs filled the room like a comforting hum, and Claire felt a deep sense of contentment enveloping her.

"She said yes, Pixel."

The cat purred louder, eyes narrowed to amber slits in his gray face. Claire leaned back against the worn velvet cushions, letting her body sink into the familiar comfort of her couch—the one splurge she'd allowed herself when she'd first signed the lease three years ago. Her studio apartment felt different somehow – not smaller as she'd first thought, but more like home. The morning light caught dust motes dancing above her fiddle-leaf fig, transforming the ordinary space into something golden and sacred, as if by stepping out into the world as her true self, she'd earned the right to truly inhabit every square inch.

She traced a finger along the hollow of her collarbone where Elena's crimson lips had been just hours before, the ghost of her jasmine perfume still lingering on Claire's skin. The memory was so vivid she could almost feel the gentle pressure, the warmth of wine-sweetened breath against her neck, the slight catch of Elena's silver necklace against her shoulder. She closed her eyes, letting the sensation ripple through her body like stones dropped in still water.

For the first time since she'd begun her transition two years and seventy-three doctor's appointments ago, Claire felt no urge to analyze or critique herself. No mental checklist of how her voice might have cracked or risen too artificially, no catalog of masculine gestures to suppress, no silent rehearsal of how to move through the world tomorrow.

More from The Glass Heel Series
by Tatiana Vixen Reyes

First Step
A single step into The Glass Heel becomes the beginning
of a journey she can never walk back.

Room 312
Behind the door of Room 312, she discovers the kind of
connection that only exists when the world is shut out.

Neon Diner
At the Neon Diner, between coffee and confession, she
discovers exactly what she's been starving for.

Sanctuary Nights
In the hush of Sanctuary Nights, she finds the safety that
finally lets her let go.